THE DARK SIDE OF THE MOON

A LESTER CAINE PRIVATE EYE NOVEL

fred berri

fred berri has won multiple 1ˢᵗ Prize Five Star Prestigious International Literary Book Awards for his novels and children's books.

***

Reader's Favorite 5 Star Award

Readers' Favorite provides professional reviews for authors and has earned the respect of renowned publishers such as Random House, Simon & Schuster and Harper Collins. Readers' Favorite also tries to help those in need by donating books and income each year to St. Jude Children's Research Hospital.

Donate: https://rb.gy/2klwd

*** *** ***

Facebook:
https://www.facebook.com/fredberriwriter/

&

Instagram-LinkedIn-"X" (formally Twitter)-Goodreads

YouTube:
https://www.youtube.com/channel/UCiJ2VzaHJFU_MjcjnqDda6g

To subscribe for advanced special offers, bonus content, updates from the author and info on new releases,

Go To:
fredberri.com

Lester Caine Private Eye - The Dark Side of The Moon
© 2023 frederic dalberri
Publisher: frederic dalberri
Winston Salem, North Carolina

ISBN: 979-8-9855923-9-9 Print
ISBN:979-8-9985372-0-2 Ebook
LCCN: 2025906421 Library of Congress

LESTER CAINE PRIVATE EYE
THE DARK SIDE OF THE MOON

BOOK THREE OF LESTER CAINE PRIVATE EYE SERIES

(A stand-alone book)

Reader Awareness

This story is intended for a mature audience and contains adult material including coarse language, sexual content, and violence.

DEDICATION

To my wife Louisa, the love of my life, affectionately
known to many as "Lola." I will miss you forever.
"Ci vediamo quando ci vediamo."
(See you when we see you)

NOTE FROM THE AUTHOR

This story is fictional. Any names, characters, places, or situations are purely coincidental and are a "fougasse.[1]" Any similarity to real persons, living or dead, is coincidental and not intended by the author, except for historical events, historical dates, or any actual locations and facts.

This novel portrays historical places and people as accurately as possible, given the best information. Therefore, I blend fact and fiction to enhance the fictional story. Historical personage that existed stands side by side with the fictional ones who all act and speak at the author's vagary.

---

[1] Fougasse /fuːˈgɑːs/ is a term used for "fake" or not real. The word originated back in the seventeenth century to describe a fake rock that was filled with explosives during wars. Soldiers would step on these fake rocks, exploding the bomb and causing serious injury or death. So the rock being fake or not real was termed a *fougasse*. This novel is a fougasse.

"The moon reflects the love of your heart to poets—

but hides the dark side few ever see."

fred berri

FOREWORDS

Storytelling has been one of the biggest parts of my life since I was four years old. From being that 80's kid plopped in front of the TV absorbing life-changing stories like Star Wars, Indiana Jones, The Goonies and Back To The Future to the 90s teenager studying The Godfather, Taxi Driver, Pulp Fiction and Heat, seeking out new characters and adventures was a deep part of my life experience.

As an adult, the works of fred berri conjure up that same childhood feeling of wonder, a rare commodity in the 2020s. Rich, deep characters mixed with intricate stories had me loving fred's previous novels, like Cousin's Bad Blood, Ten Cents A Dance and Lester Caine: Private Eye.

It comforts me to know there's one author that will bring out that childhood joy, sucked into the incredible worlds and characters fred has created for all of us to enjoy!

JON DEINER
OUTPOST 32 PRODUCTIONS
HOLLYWOOD, CALIFORNIA

Being a professional narrator for audio books and a music engineer, working with Fred's dynamic stories, has outgunned all the others in my career. I had to speak in the voices of Polish Jews, Germans—Everyone, from the Bronx to the Bowery and Italian lines of dialogue in his previous Lester Caine novels I never thought would be in my playbook. Fred encouraged me and I became the voice of one of Fred Berri's most iconic characters, Lester Caine (and his Cohorts). With The Dark Side of the Moon, whether you have the text version or the audio version, there will be thrills, spills and a twist at every turn hunting the murderer of film star, Ruby Russell—from the beaches of Florida to the glitter of Hollywood.

DENVER RISLEY
THE CHURCH STUDIO
TULSA, OKLAHOMA
WWW.FACEBOOK.COM/DCRSILVER

PROLOGUE

Crime scenes are three dimensional—the floor, the walls, and the ceiling. The examination of a crime scene is only as good as the leading officer's ability to analyze and preserve the scene, effectively preventing the loss and contamination of evidence. Cops themselves compromise most crime scenes, not just by being the first there, but by investigators who follow. Lester cringed as he recalled his first on-scene investigation as a uniformed cop.

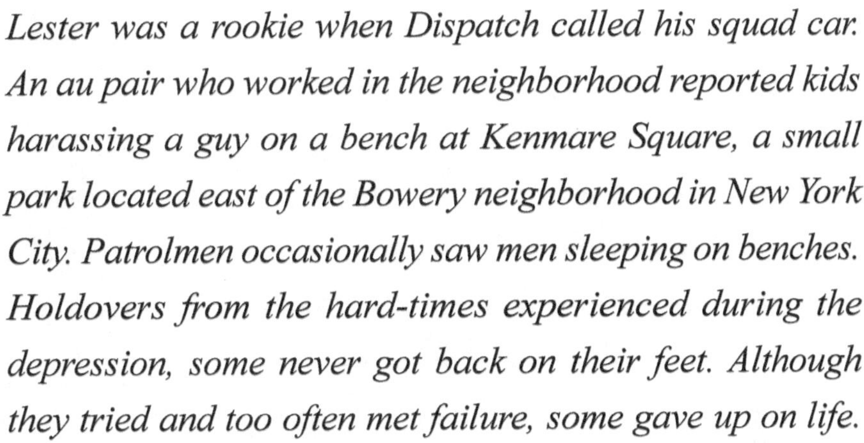

Lester was a rookie when Dispatch called his squad car. An au pair who worked in the neighborhood reported kids harassing a guy on a bench at Kenmare Square, a small park located east of the Bowery neighborhood in New York City. Patrolmen occasionally saw men sleeping on benches. Holdovers from the hard-times experienced during the depression, some never got back on their feet. Although they tried and too often met failure, some gave up on life.

Many poor saps dressed to go to work each morning but wound up on the soup lines or sleeping on the street. Years later, cops still saw stragglers known as the Bowery Bums.

Getting out of the cop car, Lester saw a guy on the bench. Off to the side, a woman was jawing at the beat cop.

"Says she saw a bunch of kids throwing pebbles at the guy." The cop addressed Lester with some relief, pointing the woman toward Lester.

"Little savages, that's what they are. Attacking a sleeping man. What's the world coming to?" The woman worked in the area for one of the fashionable families— owners of businesses and the wealthy, elite of society. Armed with her umbrella, she had chased the kids away.

The man lay motionless, dressed in a suit, a newspaper covered his face. Lester remembered walking over to him.

"Hey buddy." He poked the sleeper with his nightstick. Once, twice, three pokes and nothing. Lester used the stick to flip the newspaper away and stumbled back. Half of the guy's face was missing. Brains, splintered bone fragments, blood, gray gook, slime and other unrecognizable substances fed the maggots crawling in and out of his nose, ears, and mouth. Flies buzzed and danced over the one eye that remained. Lester heaved his breakfast all over the crime scene, adding to the gore. Yeah, he knew firsthand how that crime scene got contaminated.

Since that experience, Lester had become desensitized, many times using dark humor and jokes at the scene—like the murder committed in a bar. Stepping away from the body, he turned to his partner. *"You know, Gus, when my Uncle Frank died, he wanted his ashes to be buried in his favorite beer mug. So, he became Frank-in-Stein."*

There were no walls to the current crime scene. The ceiling was the sky. Assisted by the bejeweled glittering sparks of stars ignited by the angels, the full moon illuminated the darkness. A wondrous southern sky before sunrise, before the sun's heat rays and light could scorch the earth from ninety-three million miles away in eight minutes, twenty seconds flat.

During the examination of a crime scene, investigators collect any available testimonial and physical evidence. Unlike the stink and mess of interior crimes, this floor yielded Hexanal—the enticing aroma of freshly cut grass on a manicured lawn. Between the sky and the lawn, in front of the world, spectators gawked at the naked body of Ruby Russell, top box office leading lady, a mega star who'd lit up the silver screen in dozens of movies.

The news of Ruby Russell's demise would circle the globe, awakening movie buffs everywhere, gaining in momentum and increasing in volume with each repetition, eventually eclipsing Marie, the biggest, loudest, and favorite bell in the Bell Tower rung by Quasimodo, the hunchback of Notre Dame. This news clip would not issue a call to hype a Red-Carpet Movie Premier or an Oscar award, but reveal the death of Ruby Russell. Flash bulbs lit the night like lightning bolts, not photographing A-list actors and actresses in tailored tuxedos and designer gowns, their brilliant jewels rivaling the flashes but highlighting the body suspended from the balcony.

There was no fanfare, producers, directors or film crew. There were no eyewitnesses to interview or any apparent physical evidence. Just Ruby, naked and alone, hanging from the second story of her Palm Beach mansion.

Lester swung out of his Horizon Blue Caddy Convertible, hesitated, and drew on his cigarette. He studied *what* was before him—uniforms walking in, out, and around the premises. Reporters pressed against the fence. This was not a pristine crime scene.

He knew a day on Palm Beach didn't start until the universe directed it. On this day, the universe screamed ... Wake Up! You won't want to miss what's waiting for you.

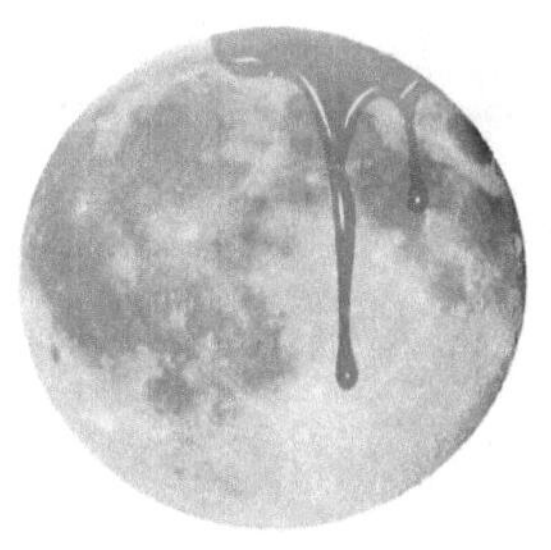

ONE

"Sorry, Sir. You can't go in there," stated a Palm Beach police officer standing at the yellow crime scene tape.

Lester Caine fumbled in his jacket pocket for his P.I. license.

"Let him through," Lieutenant Walker shouted before Lester could show his ID, his gate pass past the centurion guarding the huge wrought iron gate emblazoned with the initials "RR."

"Jesus, you would think all the uniforms would know him by now," muttered Walker.

Lester followed the sound of Walker's voice.

Lieutenant Walker, Palm Beach Police Homicide Department, followed protocol most of the time. He was, like Lester, a cop's cop. That's why they got along so well. Walker grew up in Florida. From an early age, he wanted to be a cop. The homicide detectives who came into the retail orange grove store he and his mother managed introduced him to crime detection. He listened to all the horrific, detailed gory stories related by them when they came in for their free basket of oranges and juice. He cataloged each detail of the murder, spellbound, and rehashed the case, thinking about what he would have done. The lurid headlines and speculation surrounding the discovery of two raped and murdered teenage girls in an Okeechobee canal shaped Walker's ambition. He devoured every printed word, imagined the scene where the killer left the bodies. That case led to his present position.

"Thanks for coming, Caine. I asked you here because of your experience with dead people."

"Hell, Ron, we're both in that business. The unnatural, premature death business that never goes away. It will always be here. It's sad; it's evil; it's wrong, and it pisses me off. Somebody called you here to determine if this is a homicide. Might be a suicide," Lester shrugged. "From my quick look-see, I'll go on record it's no accident. Look at this as job security, sick as it is, 'cause there will always be another, then another and another." Lester's voice held conviction.

"That's one way to look at it. I guess all those years as an NYPD homicide detective influenced you. I get what you're saying. Well, I've never asked, although I've known you for several years. Let me ask you now. How many homicides did you investigate before you retired to the soft life of a Private Eye? Bet you thought you'd retire to Paradise with all the Palm Beach Bombshells and when it rained, it would rain pennies from heaven."

"You're all wet, Ron. Yeah, the grass always looks greener on the other side of the fence, but you find out the green is because of a lot of fertilizer."

"So, you're saying there's a lot of shit spread around to make it look good here?" Walker smirked.

"Bingo. It's all bullshit. But I never tire of looking at those women you refer to as bombshells, even some in the two hundred murders in my twenty-five years in the NYPD," Lester said.

"Jesus H Christ, Caine. That's ..." He pointed his index finger and, moving it through the air, muttered while he calculated. "That's eight homicides a year you worked."

"I need your experience here. This," and Walker waved his hand at the corpse, "is going to be a real shit show. I'm not too proud to ask for help. Do you know who's hanging there for all the looky-loos and the morbidly curious to see?" Not waiting for an answer, he blurted, "It's *The* Ruby Russell. Can you believe it, Caine? Shit, I can't. She's as beautiful dead as she was in every movie I saw."

"Come on, Ron. That's because you're on the ground looking up. Wait until you see her up close."

"Well, she's right here in my piece of Palm Beach paradise. A goddamned goddess! Look around. You have my clearance."

"Where the hell is the M.E.? In this heat, she'll bake before long," Walker groused.

"*The* Ruby Russell?" Lester quietly questioned.

"I heard that, Caine. Yeah, for sure that's her—*The* Ruby Russell. Look at her. Like an angel. A beautiful, naked, dead angel. You're gonna owe me a steak dinner," Walker said.

"Why?"

"Russell's Personal Assistant immediately asked for the top private investigator in West Palm Beach. I recommended you. She wants to hire you." Turning, he shouted. "Block those goddamn reporters."

"What's this world coming to?" Walker said rhetorically. "Now they have police scanners. What'd I tell you? This is a shit show. Why don't they go over to the Colony Hotel? Maybe they could take photos of ... you know, some star like Judy Garland, Frank Sinatra, or maybe the Duke and Dutchess of Windsor. They could stake out Worth Avenue where some people claim they spotted Clark Gable with a dame on his arm."

"Are you joking? While Ruby Russell hangs naked in mid-air like a defrocked angel? Palm Beach would need snow and freeze over for the newshounds to leave the scene you have here. And you know that ain't ever gonna happen. Look at the frenzy, Ron. Yelling questions, jumping up and down, desperately trying to push past the barricades. Photographers are snapping as many photos as fast as they can, hoping to get the picture that authenticates that naked corpse is Ruby Russell. Did you see who's right up front?" Lester said.

"I did. Helen Tilly, your favorite crime reporter. She's yelling your name over and over and over–like she's having an orgasm in your bed."

"At least the Miami Journal is a reputable newspaper. She usually gets the facts and reports them straight," Lester said.

"That broad's reputation carries a smear from that rag paper, *The Yellow Press,* and her past association with them. You should remember them, Lester. You caught that slug stringer who calls himself a news photographer snapping pictures of murdered Judge Vanderbilt's widow Lorraine sunbathing in the nude. Remember? You almost drowned him in her pool."

"I wanted to drown the son-of-a-bitch. So, that's why they still call her The Rag Doll Queen. Tilly's a good-looking broad. I can see the doll part. I wouldn't mind her calling out my name in bed, for real," Lester said.

"She sure is a Palm Beach bombshell."

Walker yelled at a detective walking by. "Is the M.E. here yet?"

"So, Ron, you really called me here by proxy, eh? I'll still buy you that steak dinner."

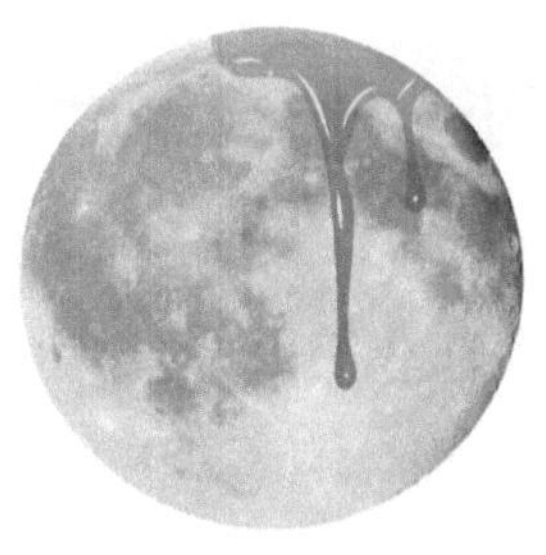

TWO

| THE CRIME SCENE

Time to get down to business, Lester thought. Positioning himself directly under Ruby's feet, he looked up. He estimated her feet were at least ten feet above his head. The second floor was approximately twenty feet, allowing a drop of ten feet. His eyes traveled up from her feet. You were *a true blond, Angel. Flying too high and somebody clipped your wings, didn't they?*

He took his time, as he always did when he was the lead detective at a crime scene. He knew it's what you don't see that is as important as what you see. There were no footprints, cigarette butts, gum or candy wrappers. No ruts, not one blade of grass out of place. Just that heady scent of freshly cut grass dug up fond memories of childhood summers—growing up in the Bronx, the public picnic park, sandlot baseball, fire hydrants turned on by the fire department to keep the neighborhood kids busy and away from mischief, Italian ices, stick ball and daylight savings time. Living and working in Palm Beach was like that ... every day was summer. *Wishes come true even when they happen decades later and thousands of miles away.*

"Tell me. What is your name?" Lester questioned the Mexican man who tended the lawn and garden. His faded clothes had seen a better day. The wide brim of his straw hat shaded his leathered face from the sun, and he wiped sweat from his brow with a large bandana. A gold cross symbolic of deeply embedded beliefs handed down through generations hung around his neck, visible only when he removed the bandana to wipe the sweat from his brow. A small man, about five feet five, he came up to Lester's shoulders. He appeared old and wrinkled. Two-day's growth of beard shadowed his chin. Lester thought he was proud of a big brush mustache.

"My name, Miguel González, Señor," he said in broken English.

"When did you first see Miss Russell?" Lester asked him, since he had discovered her body hanging.

"Oh, Señor Policia, I am busy. You know? I doing my job – I minding my business. I have to start the lawn, the hedges and flowers. Me no see Miss Russell." Hesitating, taking his hat off, he made the sign of the cross, lifting the symbol he wore to his lips. "Jesu Cristo. Maybe I mowing the lawn and got closer to ... you know ... her." Again, hesitating, he removed his hat, made the sign of the cross. Mumbling, "Jesu Cristo," he kissed his gold cross by rote. "She has everything, Señor. Why she do that?"

"I'll ask the questions. You answer."

"Si, Si, Señor. Perdóname. She was real nice lady boss. She come to the pool with her robe. She no take off until I finish," he said in his deep Spanish accent.

"Oh, you've seen her without clothes, naked?" Lester questioned.

"Señor, me no stare. She wait for me to leave. Then naked."

"You must look if you know she is naked," Lester said, putting his hand on the man's shoulder. "Don't lie to me, Miguel. God sees."

"Si, Señor. She is muy hermosa," hanging his head with guilt.

Lester paused for a moment and thought of the occasional sex he had with the widow, Lorraine Vanderbilt. He had helped capture the Judge's killer. Lorraine always reclined on a chaise by her pool, naked, drinking martinis, reading, and smoking her Pall Malls.

"So, nothing out of the ordinary? You didn't see any strangers or cars or activity going on?"

"No, Señor. I say same things to the other official de policia."

"What time did you start work?"

"I get here before and start at 6 a.m. I don't see nothing, like you say. The sun, you know, too early. It no show its face," he said.

"If the sun did not show its face, how do you work in the dark?"

"Oh, Señor, I work in the shed, get everything to work. I put tools in wheelbarrow, fill machine with petro. When the sun shows its face, I go out and start."

"Do you ever see anyone in the house with her or going into the house or leaving? A man, woman, any parties? Don't lie to me. By talking to me, you are under oath to God." Lester used Mr. Gonzalez's faith. *Blind faith*, but obvious faith.

"No, Señor. I no go in house. I no see like you say—coming or going. Miss Ruby have inside help. I report to inside lady boss, only her," he said, swiping the bandana across his face.

"Who is she—the lady boss? What's her name? What's her job?"

"Miss Amélie, Señor. I tell her what I need for the garden. I know more nothing. I have work to do. I go to work now?"

"In a minute. Do you know her last name?"

"No, Señor. Only Miss Amélie. I go now?"

"Yes, you can go, but you can't go back to work. This is a crime scene. Do you understand? You can't go into the shed or near the house. It's best if you go home. I'll speak with ...," and he scanned his notes, "Miss Amélie for you." Lester assured him he would be paid.

Gonzalez furrowed his brow, tilting his head with a quizzical look, questioning. "Crime, Señor?"

Lester ignored his half-baked question. "One more thing. Where do you live? What's your address?"

"Oh, Señor, no come my casa. I live not so nice. My wife asustada. How you say scared like cat? She sick, no work. I only work. I'm here ten years for Señora. I need job."

"Okay, okay, I understand. Scaredy-cat," Lester chuckled. "You called her Señora. Do you know the Señora's husband?"

"Oh, no, Señor. I not know. I call her Señora ... receptor. I no see marido."

"I get it, respect for her. I won't come, but I still need your address," Lester said, pointing heavenward, then to his eyes to remind Mr. Gonzalez from his mouth to God's ears and watching.

Lester looked up at Ruby Russell, hearing the González's words. '*Why she do that? She have everything.*' Then, "Christ, why haven't they taken her down? Where the hell is the M.E.?"

THREE

| LET THE FORENSICS BEGIN

"Doc, you could at least have brought coffee and donuts in the time it took you to get here, for Christ's sake. What did you do, take the scenic route along A1A?" Lieutenant Walker's snarky comment was a sign of his agitation. "She's going to cook out here." Walker scowled at the M.E.

"Calm down, Lieutenant. She's not the only stiff I'll add to my refrigerators today. Besides, it's just 7 a.m. The sun hasn't turned on its oven yet. She'll be gone soon. I see your fan club. Do they follow you everywhere you go these days?" The M.E. snickered. Adding a jab to Walker, he waved at the group of newspaper reporters.

Ignoring him, Walker motioned to the balcony. "Let's go. You, too, Doc, and your assistant. Let's pull her in."

"Are the crime scene men done with the forensics on the balcony?" asked the M.E.

"They've been done, except for looking for fingerprints on the rope and more photos of her close up. We couldn't move the body until your highness arrived."

"Caine, let's go. Upstairs to the balcony," Walker shouted. "The Prince of Darkness is finally here."

Lester counted each step of the sweeping Grand Staircase, noting its exact proportions and precision. He admired the intricately carved handrail of the finest mahogany wood, smooth to his hand, although covered with fingerprint dust. *This place was immaculate ... before the sweepers. Maybe they'll get some fresh prints.* This precision led him to a new place and time. The staircase had more significance than just the mundane means of getting to the second floor. It would be an instrument for revealing the innocence of an angel or the guilt of the long arm that held the scythe of death. Six beautiful, signed paintings of Cillespi hung on the staircase walls. Each nude, six of them, exhibited a gold plate with the description: *Afternoon Rest,* easily worth thousands of dollars.

Ruby Russell was not enjoying afternoon rest. She was at eternal rest. Why was she hanging from a rope in her own home, naked and dead?

The M.E.'s assistant took a long-handled grapple hook from his bag of tricks. He extended the pole to reach the rope, easing it to the railing. All four men waited silently to lift Ruby's body up and over the railing. She twirled faster and faster with each tug of the rope, bringing her closer to the railing, like a child's toy ballerina, stopping only when they reached out to prevent her from colliding with the stucco wall. Boldly, her bulging eyes stared at each one of them.

"Jesus H. Christ. Hurry up. She's watching us," Lieutenant Walker grunted as he leaned out to guide the rope.

"She's not staring at you. She's dead," said the M.E. "There's a lack of oxygen. The eyes bulge because the cells around the eyes shrink, causing fluid changes in the tissues and cells that hinge the eyeballs. The congestion pushes the eyeballs from the socket and ..."

PULL!" Walker grunted.

"Ease her down, fellas. On the sheet," Lieutenant Walker commanded.

"Holy shit," exclaimed the M.E.'s assistant. "That's Ruby Russell."

"Sure as there's fuzz on a peach," Lieutenant Walker said.

"Peach fuzz protects the fruit from insects," the M.E. said.

There was an awkward silence among them as they stared, admiring her naked body. The M.E. closed her eyes ever so gently.

"That's not like any peach fuzz I've ever seen," said the assistant, staring at Ruby's breasts, moving slowly to her painted toes.

"Nothing protected her, Doc. Un ange passse," Lester said.

"What? You said something, Lester?" Walker asked.

"I said, "nothing protected her.""

"No, no, after that," Walker asked.

"Un ange passse. It's French. An angel is passing. One of my ex-wives was French. My mother does tarot cards and reaches the divine on the other side," Lester added.

"What say you, Doc? And not in French or any hocus pocus of ghosts and spirits and those crazy cards Caine's mother plays with," Walker said.

The M.E. carefully gripped Ruby's head, slightly turning it.

"Well, she's dead," he said, waiting for his hardened humor to sink into the men whose eyes were glued to the body.

"No shit, Doc," Walker said, looking up. "Har de har har. They teach you that in medical school?"

"And I would not be surprised if Lester's mother connects with her spirit," he said, shrugging off Walker's criticism.

"Now you're a comedian? Maybe we should have called Lester's mother here to ask her why the fuck she's hanging here," Walker said.

"She's stiff and cold because of the chemical changes in the muscle fibers. See what happens when I put pressure here and here on her lower extremities? When I release my thumb, the marks are permanent caused by the blood settling. If I applied pressure and the marks did not show, it would say something different. I'd say she's dead at least eight hours."

Lester wrote every detail he heard in his notebook, ignoring Walker's comment about his mother, Pamela, who he knows nothing about. He looked at his watch for the current time.

"What about the rope, Doc?" Lester asked.

"It was a long drop, broke her neck. That would cause near immediate loss of consciousness and death would occur rapidly thereafter. The ligature shows blackening of the skin, which is friction burn," he added.

"No defensive wounds?" Lester asked.

"What you see. Some likely from swinging and hitting the wall of the house."

What about the rope itself, Doc?" Lester repeated.

"It looks like common macrame cotton rope to me, but the crime scene boys can tell you more. Seems like several strands of cord separated into sections and then twisted around each other to form a thicker, stronger rope. You can get it at any hardware store. Did you know scientists found sketches by Leonardo da Vinci of a rope making machine from the 1400s? No one ever developed the machine. The man was a genius!"

"Yeah, maybe so, but did he ever solve a murder?" Walker growled with considerable impatience.

The M.E. ignored the Lieutenant.

"It's an unsophisticated simple slip knot that did her in. I'll know more when I get her on my table. We'll screen for drugs and booze. I know, I know," he sighed. "You want the report yesterday. I'll call you Lieutenant. Caine, you'll have to get my findings from Walker," he said.

"My God. She is so beautiful. Just look at her. Like ... a Venus de Milo," the M.E.'s assistant said.

"Put your eyes back in your head, kid. I'll grant you she's like a marble statue—stiff with rigor and cold like marble." Lieutenant Walker grinned, effectively emasculating the Doc's assistant.

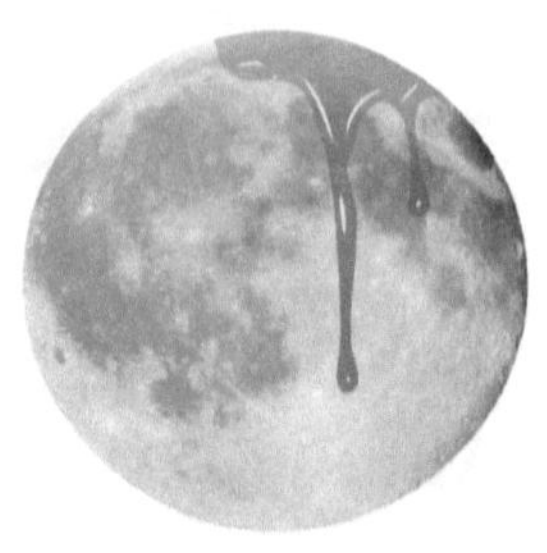

FOUR

| A NEEDED VOICE

Lester scoured the area, inch by inch, room by room, the same procedure he followed at every crime scene, looking for the seen and the unseen, for what spoke to him and what didn't, what was ordinary and what was out of place. He never dismissed the small things, the seemingly inconsequential things. He listened for some clue Ruby Russell might give him in her silence.

Lester was an advocate for the dead. Someone had to be their voice. It didn't matter who they had been in life or what they did. They were all human beings who had not deserved to have their lives taken from them. His last case, Kurt Voker, the Nazi War Criminal, was an exception to his victim advocate stance. An envelope taped under a nightstand drawer at the crime scene of Desmond Vanderbilt, a murdered judge, had led him and his associate, Gloria Saville, to an international manhunt a few months back.

Now, he took down wall paintings, removed photos of Ruby with Hollywood's finest out of their frames. He rummaged through drawers, looked underneath and behind them, emptied shoe boxes in her closet, turned pockets of her clothing inside out, just like he had in Argentina. That scrutiny had led to the discovery of Leopold Israel Rabinowitz, the name of a Jew from the death camps whose identity Kurt Voker stole to help him escape Europe after World War 2. Lester had left nothing undisturbed then and did the same now in Ruby Russell's mansion.

He remembered the homicides he led over his twenty-five years with the NYPD—hookers, drug dealers, gamblers, mobsters, families, even cops, and elected officials. Some guilty of crimes, some innocent, including his father's unsolved murder in a back-alley crap game that motivated him to become a cop.

Lester knew he had to be the victim's voice, although a few didn't deserve his dedication, ever. During his career, there may have been victims who were guilty and deserved the death penalty, but a vigilante or a psychopath shouldn't make that decision. He paused his search to unravel his thoughts. *Ah, bullshit. Some exceptions deserved what vigilante justice had done.* Ruby Russell did not deserve this end. He knew she hadn't died by her own hand. What stuck in his craw was the absence of a suicide note. No diary or letters. A *famous screen star, a sex symbol, would have fan mail, evidence of stalker...something. What am I missing?*

Hands grabbed Lester underneath his armpits and clasped around the back of his neck to lock him in position, head forced forward. He pushed backward, hoping to hit something and knock this phantom off balance. The thud was loud, knocking against the wall. Lester's foe stumbled, losing his grip. They scrambled to their feet, and Lester faced his opponent. Eye to eye, each pondered the other's next move. Lester's training surfaced. He struck a defensive stance. His opponent, small, Asian, held his position on the cusp of attack like a viper rising slowly for the strike. Neither spoke.

His opponent's stance showed ancient martial arts knowledge. He advanced, thrusting a blow, missing Lester's jaw, but caught his left ear, causing a deafening loud shrill ringing. Lester concentrated on the protocol from the great Kung Fu masters: attack the arm that attacks you; but in a street fight, protocol goes to hell and there is no time for strategy. Lester grabbed the Asian's arm, pulling it toward him and to his side to straighten it. The stranger fell to the floor. Turning, he scissored Lester's legs, bringing them both down. They rolled over and over to the top of the stairs. Lester glanced to his side, resolved he wasn't falling to the bottom. Lester punched his assailant's eye with his thumb, grabbing his throat with his other hand. His opponent-rolled and jumped to his feet, aiming a kick at Lester's side. Lester seized the move to grab the Asian's leg and throw him to the floor, gaining enough advantage to regain his feet. The Asian man was agile and fast. He thrust out his arm to catch Lester's neck, but Lester deflected the oncoming blow, snapping his hand upward like a knife's edge, striking the core of his opponent's neck, impacting his carotid nerve, and dropping his blood pressure. Lester's foe fell to the floor, ending the fight.

"Mr. Caine? Mr. Caine?" a voice sounded, sending a wave of sound through the air like a pageboy walking through the lobby of a hotel: *'Paging Lester Caine. Paging Lester Caine.'*

"That would be me. Who are you and why are you looking for me?" Lester answered matter-of-factly, placing a foot on the man's back, holding him prone. He removed the gun sticking out of his attacker's jacket pocket and cuffed him.

"Oh, my God! Oh, my God! What happened to Lei? What have you done?" Her voice rose, aggravating the ringing in his ear.

"Lei, are you alright?" She cried, rushing to the fallen man, trying to push Lester aside.

"Who are you? Who is he?" Lester said.

"I'm Miss Russell's Personal Assistant, Amélie. He is Lei Chang, Miss Russell's bodyguard. And you ... " She paused, looking at Lester, then at the fallen man. "Are you Lester Caine?"

"I am. Not much of a bodyguard, was he?" Lester gestured to the balcony, then to the man on the floor.

"I *was* Ruby Russell's assistant." Rivulets of mascara smeared her cheeks. "Lei will be, okay?"

"He'll survive. Just a blow to the throat and a bruised ego. You'll be alright too. Take deep breaths." He handed her his pocket square to wipe her face.

"Thank you, Mr. Caine. Male chivalry isn't dead. You are a gentleman."

Lester's eyebrow lifted. *She recovered quickly if she could flirt.* Still, *this broad could teach Gloria some romanticisms.*

"I mean it. The war changed people more than anyone will admit. Hardened them. Who can blame them? Hollywood is not what you see on the silver screen. Ruby was beautiful, Mr. Caine. I loved her. We were like sisters. Oh my God! I can't believe what she did, and Chang ... on the floor in handcuffs. I'm not feeling well."

"Sit next to your friend here." Lester instructed. "If you're planning a lifetime with this guy, not to worry. He'll come around. Sit."

"Thank you. I'm alright. Lei? No, never," countering Lester's assumption. "It's, it's, you know, I'm just..." lowering herself slowly. Lester offered his hand to lend support. "Please, Mr. Caine, can you take the handcuffs off Lei. He must have thought you were, I don't know. Please take off the cuffs."

"In due time. See, your Mr. Chang is coming around," Lester assured her.

"Lei is ... was a stuntman in martial art films in Hong Kong. He came to Hollywood when the heroes of Shanghai films were often rebellious. The Cantonese versions of these characters are chivalrous and upheld Confucian values. That's when Lei came to Hollywood to pursue a career as a fighting hero, not as a flowery leading man. Miss Russell saw his films and as a stuntman on set. She hired him as a bodyguard. Miss Russell's attorney told me to cooperate with the police, provide whatever they need or may ask for. Lieutenant Walker suggested I hire you. He said you're the best Private Investigator he ever knew, the caliber of Charlie Chan,[2] always solving the case."

"Amélie, you realize Charlie Chan is a fictional character?"

"Yes, Mr. Caine. I do. I've seen both actors, Warner Oland and Sidney Toler, on set when Miss Russell was shooting in the next studio. On the set, Ruby saw Lei."

"There's a big difference between Hong Kong movies and Hollywood, Amélie. Mr. Chang, in Hollywood, is on the fringe and may never be a Hollywood martial arts hero."

"One can hope, yes, Mr. Caine?" Her smug demeanor struck a nerve. "Lieutenant Walker also told me about your service with the New York Police Department. I've read about the headline cases you solved. Will you take this case, Mr. Caine? Please. We, the studio, her attorneys

---

[2] Charlie Chan is a fictional Honolulu police detective created for a series of mystery novels and movies.

will pay you whatever it takes. The world needs to know the truth," she said. Her manner made Lester wonder if she aspired to be an actress.

The dynamics shifted with, 'We … will pay you whatever it takes.' Music replaced the ringing in Lester's ears. It would take a bundle of scratch to resolve this mystery.

Taking out his notebook, Lester asked, "What's your last name?"

«Dubois, Mr. Caine. Amélie Dubois.»

"Ah, French. Qui? Bonjour, mademoiselle."

"My accent gave me away? Do you speak French, Mr. Caine?"

"Yes, your accent. No, I don't speak French, but I'm familiar with the accent. One of my ex-wives was French."

"You are unmarried? Excuse me, Mr. Caine." She trailed off, abruptly stopping like someone suddenly aware of a burning building's edge, deciding whether to jump. His handsome features—hazel eyes, strong jawline, and a prominent cleft chin—attracted her.

Lester knew this broad didn't buy off the rack and was more than a see-through negligee beauty in a girly magazine. She exuded class, the kind only gained by Hollywood grooming. His libido heated momentarily. *Should I consider her invitation?*

Chang moaned and struggled to sit up.

"What the hell?" Tension surfaced as he tugged at the cuffs. "Get these off me. Who the hell are you? My throat. Why did you do that? You could have killed me." Chang's gravelly voice came through his coughs.

"Sit down. Be quiet," Lester said, smiling at Amélie. "If I wanted to kill him, I would have."

He turned to Chang. "Promise to be calm, and I'll take the cuffs off. I'm Lester Caine, a private investigator. I'll take the case, Miss Dubois, but the Palm Beach Police and Lieutenant Walker are primary."

"Thank you, Mr. Caine. Yes, I know that. I, the studio ... we need everyone, private or police, to get to the bottom of this tragedy and find the reason Ruby would do this thing. Please, it's okay to address me by my first name. I would prefer it. In this country, everyone calls me Frenchie. So please, Mr. Caine, Frenchie."

"Alright, Frenchie, I'll take the case. My attorney will send over the Agreement for signatures. Let's sit somewhere to talk."

"Enough bullshit chit-chat. The honeymoon is over. Help me up and take these cuffs off," Chang said.

"Will you be a good boy?" Lester's taunt landed like a punch to the stomach, further deflating Chang's ego.

"Yeah. It's alright now I know who you are." Chang agreed, trying to save face.

Lester released him, ejecting the bullet from the handgun's slide and emptying the loaded magazine clip from Chang's roscoe onto the floor before he handed it to him.

"That wasn't necessary," Chang said.

"Just a precaution my arms instructor preached years ago," Lester said.

"What the hell is all this commotion?" Walker yelled, charging up the stairs with two of his officers in tow. He saw Lester remove the handcuffs from Chang and stared at the mascara smeared on Amélie's face.

"All under control, Lieutenant. Right, Mr. Chang?" Lester said, avoiding and misdirecting Walker's question. "Ron, have you met Amélie Dubois and Lei Chang? Miss Russell's assistant and her bodyguard. I think we need a warrant for the gardener's house, just to sweep out all the corners."

"Yeah, I can get that. What about this?" Walker pointed to the pair at hand.

"Under control, Ron. Isn't that right, Mr. Chang?"

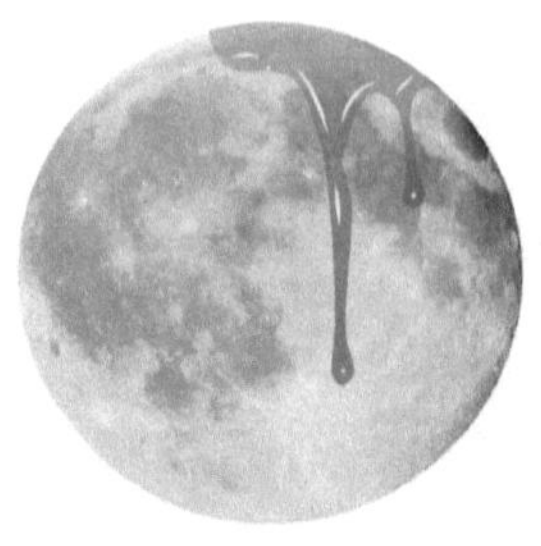

FIVE

Lester reached out to Lester Caine Investigations Associate and licensed gun toting private eye, Gloria Saville. "Drop whatever you're doing and hightail it to 10451 South Dunbar Road, Palm Beach, Florida."

Lester introduced Amélie Dubois to his associate, who at one time was a highly experienced army intelligence officer. Her skills ranged from master cryptologist to accomplished disguise artist. She currently honed her artistry during summer stock playhouse performances, earning her the nickname Scarecrow.

"I'm sorry we have to meet under such..." Gloria began.

"Horror, Miss Saville. Horror. I have no words," Amélie said, her voice cracking, her hands trembling.

"I'm sorry for your loss, Amélie. Truly. You were Miss Russell's personal assistant?" Gloria said.

"Yes, yes, I feel I still am. We were like sisters. I've been with Ruby for many years. I do so many things and there are arrangements to make. Ruby is Hollywood's beloved. She must look perfect. Her makeup artists will take care of that. I must plan a memorial service. I must get her back to California," Amélie said through sobs.

"We'll be brief," Gloria promised. "Tell me, how did you find out about Miss Russell?"

"Miss Saville, I told Mr. Caine, my acquaintances know me as Frenchie. So, everyone doesn't know Amélie. It is best to keep Frenchie."

Gloria raised an eyebrow at the implied reprimand, exchanging a look with Lester.

"Well, Miss Saville, Miguel's yelling, banging and frantic ringing of the doorbell required attention. Miguel is our gardener," she explained.

"I met him," Lester said. "Hmm. He failed to tell me that. What time was it?"

"I don't know, Mr. Caine. I was yet asleep. Rarely do I start my day until seven ish. That's when my alarm goes off. I go downstairs, grab a cup of coffee, and review

Miss Russell's schedule for the day before I shower and dress. I must wait until 9 a.m. to call California. Because of the time difference—three hours, you see?"

Gloria nodded.

"Her agent and the studio people are awake and buzzing by that time—

6 a.m. there. Some studio people are on set as early as 5 a.m. for make-up, wardrobe, rehearsals, and all. It depends."

"Okay, so Miguel is yelling, whatever. Do you speak Spanish? What happened next?" Lester asked, firing questions at her.

"No, no, I don't speak Spanish, Mr. Caine."

"How did you know what he was saying?" Gloria asked.

"I have to think a moment. This is too much. My poor head is spinning. Ah! He was pointing, yelling, mixing Spanish and English, making the sign of the cross. He was repeating some mumble jumble, calling on Jesus and urging me to come with him. I hurried out to the yard, trying to find the source of his agitation."

"What happened next?" Gloria asked.

"Then? Then what? I looked up and saw ... I must have passed out on the lawn. When I opened my eyes, Miguel was fanning me with his hat. He tapped my face, saying my name over and over. I do not know how long

I was unconscious. He helped me stand. Somehow, I made it to the house and called the police. I just got off the phone with Miss Russell's attorney and agent before you found me. I had to tell them before the story broke. Everyone is in shock."

"Do you see the news people out front? They're like Piranhas in a feeding frenzy. Her agent and public relations people will issue a statement to the studio stockholders and to the public. What a mess. Oh, my god, my god."

"Would you like some water?" Gloria asked.

"No, maybe something stronger? I need a minute."

"You told Lester you told this to Lieutenant Walker. Is that correct?" Gloria asked.

"Yes. He knows all this. Why must I rehash it all?"

"It may seem redundant to you, Amélie. Excuse me, Miss Frenchie. You spoke to the Lieutenant and Mr. Caine. You hired Lester Caine Investigations, correct? We've found that sometimes more details come to mind during follow-up interviews," Gloria said.

"Details you may not have remembered the first time because of your shock at seeing Miss Russell," Lester added.

"I understand. Okay, Mr. Caine. I will cooperate fully. Anything ... like I said," her eyes met Gloria's with a challenge.

"Did Lieutenant Walker tell you that you have to make a formal statement at the police station?" Lester said.

"Why?" she snapped. "I just told you the same statement I gave to him." She stiffened and glared at him.

"I understand you're upset. I would be too," Gloria said, commiserating with her. "But the law requires you to comply when there's an untimely death. You must make a formal statement to the police, which they will record. There will probably be a clerk present to take more notes. Speaking of notes, did you find a note, letters? What about a diary?" Gloria said.

"No, nothing," Amélie snapped. Her annoyance growing with each repetition of the same questions requiring her answers. "Ruby didn't keep a diary. She feared it would get out and ruin her Hollywood super stardom."

Lester recalled Plato's insight, thinking, *'All suicides are equally bad, but rather that each case is individual and may be judged as permissible according to circumstance.'*

He and Gloria knew revealing diary entries were no longer an issue. Ruby Russell was not going back to California soon. Not until this investigation fully and positively determined Ruby Russell's true cause of death, ruled it either suicide or murder, would the authorities release her body. This is unbeknown to most victims' families. Amélie, Ruby's immediate family, her publicist, attorneys, and her production studio, would have to practice patience.

"What can you tell me about Mr. González?" Gloria asked.

"Miguel the gardener? He is what he is and does. Nothing more. A humble man, he has worked for Miss Russell for years. Even when we go to Hollywood, he continues, never missing a day of work, rain or shine. He's a hard worker. That's it. That's all I know about him or his family."

"Okay. Thank you." Gloria's cool acceptance dismissed Mr. González. "That's all ... for now."

"Miss Dubois, a uniform and squad car are on the way to take you and Mr. Chang to the station," Lester said.

"Why? Why is this happening? How can I go on? What am I going to do? I feel sick. I think I'm going to throw up," Amélie mumbled.

"Miss Saville, we're here," Walker said, approaching with two uniformed officers. "We're ready to escort everyone to the station. We have the housekeeper in a car already."

He turned to his men. "Put them in separate interview rooms," he reminded them as they escorted Amélie and Chang to the car. There was no mistaking the command in Walker's voice.

INTERROGATION

"Where are Frenchie and the housekeeper?" Chang's eyes narrowed as he demanded an answer.

"Now, who is Frenchie?" Walker asked.

"That's Miss Dubois. We all know her as Frenchie."

"They're in another interview room doing the same thing you're here for," Walker stated.

"And what's that?"

"To ask you some questions about..."

"About Ruby? She hung herself. You saw her. It's terrible. Why would she do that? I can't imagine ever putting a rope around my neck, can you, Lieutenant?"

"Every time I wear a necktie, but I'll ask the questions, Mr. Chang."

"Sure. Fire away. I guess, as you say, ask some questions. I'm ready."

"How long did you work for Miss Russell?"

"About three years. You ever see her movies, Lieutenant?"

"When was the last time you saw Miss Russell ... alive?" Walker asked, ignoring Chang's question. Suspects commonly tried to throw off his concentration, misdirect or try to lead the procedure. Walker was damn sure that would not happen, not in his interview room.

"About nine or nine thirty. After everyone left and I did a security check."

"What does your security check comprise, Mr. Chang?"

"C'mon, Lieutenant, you're a cop. You know what has to be checked."

"Yes, I know, but I'd like to confirm we're on the same page. And the faster you answer my questions, the faster you'll be able to leave."

"After everyone is secluded in their rooms, I walk around the property. When I return, I check the windows and doors, make sure they're locked."

"Walk around the property? Outside?"

"Yes."

"And..."

"What? That's what I do every night."

"Were you drinking that night?"

"Well, sure. We all were."

"We all were? Who exactly are we all?"

"Everyone at dinner. Amélie told me she gave you the guest list."

"How much did you drink?"

"I don't know. I had wine with dinner. After we went to the drawing room, we had cocktails and talked."

"What did you talk about?"

"Just everyday shit, you know."

"Actually, Mr. Chang, I don't know. That's why we are here in this room. So...?"

"The weather, anybody's travel plans, Ruby's upcoming film. It was going to be different for her, another romance flick, but with a twist."

"I don't understand."

"Yeah, you'd have to be one of us to get it. A romantic suspense movie with a few stunts for me."

"Do you get paid extra for your stunts, Mr. Chang, on top of your security detail for Miss Russell?"

"Yes, of course. I'm a member of SAG. It's required to be in the movies."

"Of course. The Screen Actors Guild. How many drinks did you have?"

"I don't know, maybe three or four."

"Straight or on the rocks?"

"Neat."

"I like mine that way, too. No ice."

"Are we done yet?"

"Almost. After everyone left and you did your security check ... Ah, when you went outside, did you leave the door ajar?"

"Yes."

"Why?"

"Took some ribbing for a while when I locked myself out once. Almost broke my hand banging on the door before the housekeeper heard me and let me in. It was a big joke for days."

"What windows did you check?"

"Just the first level windows. I don't go into the bedrooms on the second floor."

"Hell of a lot of windows and doors on the first floor. Must take a while. I'd wish the place was a tract bungalow after a few drinks."

Chang nodded.

"Did you go straight to your room?" Walker continued.

"No," he hesitated. "I got another drink, then went to my room."

"So, that's what, your fifth drink?"

"I was not counting."

"You said you had four after dinner besides the wine. That would make five. How much wine did you have at dinner?"

"Maybe two glasses."

"Now you've had two glasses of wine and five whiskey drinks. Is that correct?"

"Yeah, I guess. So, what?"

"All that booze and you still performed your security checkpoints. You have an admirable tolerance for liquor, Chang."

"Is there an alarm system?"

"Yes, but Miss Russell liked to sit on the balcony. We didn't always activate it."

"A celebrity of her magnitude and she was lax with the security system? Now, I find that strange."

Chang shrugged.

"Ever have intruders? An exuberant fan?"

"No. We have exterior alarms, fenced property, a gate. The system inside was backup."

Walker's and Chang's eyes dueled until Chang looked down.

"When did you discover Miss Russell was dead?"

"When Frenchie screamed after seeing her hanging. I just got out of the shower when I heard Frenchie."

"What are those marks on your hands and neck, Mr. Chang?"

"Ah, these are from when that Private Dick and I got into it."

"That looks like a small puncture wound on your neck. Do you have any more?"

"No!"

"Stand up, Mr. Chang, and take off your shirt."

"No."

"We can do this the easy way or the hard way. It's procedure. This officer will take some photos. Easy or hard? Your choice."

"Tā mā de húndàn. Nǐmen suǒyǒu rén,"[3] Chang's native tongue, harsh and guttural, reflected his attitude as he took off his shirt. Walker caught the drift without an interpreter. "What the hell is this, Lieutenant? Where's the light in my eyes? Your rubber hose?"

"We rarely use torture during interviews anymore. Leaves too many marks and encourages lawsuits. You should know that shit happens only in the movies." Walker replied, tongue-in-cheek. His manner calm.

"Face front. Turn left. Now right. Turn with your back to me. Hold out your hands palms up. Show me the backs of your hands. Perfect. Thank you," the uniformed officer snapped each photo. "We're good, Lieutenant.

"Get dressed. You can go ... for now, Mr. Chang. A uniform will take you back to the mansion. Don't leave town."

---

[3] "Tā mā de húndàn. Nǐmen suǒyǒu rén",- Fucking cocksuckers. All of you.

CHAPTER

SIX

| HOME OF MIGUEL GONZÁLEZ

Lester parked his Horizon Blue Cadillac at the curb in front of Miguel Gonzalez's house and cut the engine. He had raised the top of his convertible when he and Gloria entered the neighborhood, as much out of a sense of guilt as a desire to be inconspicuous. He confirmed this was the address Ruby Russell's gardener had given him during his interview.

Thousands of migrants had used whatever means they could muster to come to the United States in search of a better life for their families and themselves. Perseverance, sweat, and hard labor gave them a firm presence, while a few individuals still found it difficult to preserve their dignity. In 1942, the U.S. established the *Bracero Program,* allowing millions of Mexicans to work legally in the U.S., primarily in agriculture. American men had marched off to war, leaving a critical void in the workforce.

Left behind in the wake of their men's exodus, women flooded the labor market. For the first time, they filled roles formerly reserved for men. They worked in the fields and vineyards, dairies, factories, schools, hospitals, offices, volunteered with the Red Cross, and served in the military. And yet, there was a shortage of workers.

Miguel was in the U.S. long before the *Bracero Program,* working at Ruby Russell's Palm Beach mansion. No one ever questioned how he came to work for Ruby. He was a fixture everyone accepted.

Miguel's stucco house was plain, a small concrete cube with no architectural frills, needing repairs. It sat on a postage-stamp-size plot of ground in a neighborhood where house after house after house duplicated the one next to it. Who owned these structures that housed the migrant workers? Were they individually owned or did a consortium of the wealthy provide housing to guarantee a plentiful supply of willing workers at their beck and call? The migrants filled vacancies as gardeners, laborers, nannies, and domestics for wineries, groves, and produce farms, hotels and private homes like Ruby Russell's mansion.

Miguel had cultivated a garden in his front yard, growing vegetables that looked like photographs in a horticultural magazine. Obviously, he possessed the proverbial green thumb.

Lester knocked lightly on the door—waited. No answer. A glance revealed a bare backyard but for a wire pen and a primitive lean-to holding a few chickens.

It's a great metaphor, Lester thought. The wealthy provide housing to protect the migrant worker, so he is available when employers need him. The wire pen protects the chickens, discouraging predators so they're available to Miguel.

He used his fist to knock again ... harder. Gloria started around back when the door creaked slowly open.

"Sénor, I go back to work now?" Miguel said.

"Sí, after we come in. I have a paper giving me access to your casa," Lester said, holding up the search warrant.

"Oh, please no, Sénor," he said, trying to close the door, but Lester's foot prevented it.

Gloria pulled her gun. "Fatti da parteMiquel o sfonda la porta[4]." She glanced at Lester and shrugged. "Italian is very similar to Spanish. He understands."

Miguel hung his head and stepped aside.

Gloria blew out a deep exhale, holstering her gun. She turned to Lester in astonishment. At the table sat a paper

---

[4] Step aside Miquel or I'll break the door.

mâché figure of a woman dressed in old-fashioned, rusty black garments an old Spanish woman would wear. She would have appeared real at a brief glance.

Miguel quickly grabbed the gold crucifix hanging around his neck, kissed it, made the sign of the cross, and sighed. "Jesu Cristo, por favor, no visitors," he murmured. "Leave us por favor, solo."

"Oh ... my ... God!" Gloria exclaimed. "Good God Almighty. What the hell is this?"

"He is celebrating *The Ofrenda,*" Lester said.

"What is it? Some sort of voodoo?" Gloria asked. "In all my years, I've never..."

"Look at all the burning candles lined up in a row, the statues of saints and photos. It's *The Day of the Dead. Ofrenda* acknowledges that the soul lives beyond the body and is mobile between heaven, hell, and purgatory. The candles light a pathway for the dead. Only the dead eat on *Ofrenda.* That's why there is food in front of the ..." Lester hesitated.

"Yeah, whatever the fuck that is, or whoever the fuck she's supposed to be. I guess you know this from your mother. With her tarot card reading and communicating with the spirits. You know, we should see her about all this. How do we know she's ... it's not Ruby Russell, and he is making atonement? We don't know if she committed suicide or if it was murder."

"The photos ... look at the photos. It must be his wife," Lester said.

Miguel stood quietly, mumbling in Spanish.

"Could he be talking to her?" Gloria glared acrimoniously.

They walked into the only other room, furnished with a bed and a dresser. A small mirror hung over the dresser. Off the main room, a cubicle contained a toilet and a sink. Nothing more. Gloria rummaged quickly through the dresser drawers with a sense of pity for Miguel and shame for her part, seeing how little he had, but she had a job to do.

"Nothing here. Let him be. Let's go," Gloria whispered. "Jesus Christ ... really? How sad is this?"

"You go to work tomorrow," Lester said to Miguel.

"Sí, Gracias."

"Lester, we need to visit your mother for a tarot card reading to give us some insight about the journey we are taking."

"Visit Pamela? Why the hell not? Her tarot card readings have helped us before. I'm sure she'd like to do her black magic and stick her nose into my business again. I'll call the witch."

"Lester, it's not black magic. Her readings are spot on. She's not a witch. She has a special talent."

"Maybe, maybe not. What are witches, anyway? I don't think they ride on brooms, although I wouldn't put it past her. She was a witch the way she treated me compared with my brother Francis."

"It's not natural for a mother to bury her son. It's supposed to be the other way around. She..."

"She, nothing, Gloria. You don't know. She treated Francis like he was a god, king of the land of the blind, a fictional character with one eye to see and the other blind. He got the accordion and tap dance lessons while I had to schlep his gear and accompany him to those lessons across town on a bus. Francis was the star in silk shirts, his name in glitter on his accordion, performing in talent shows, while I tagged along, playing bodyguard, his muscle. He got the gravy, and I got the witch's icy tit. Don't preach that bullshit rationale to me. Yes, Francis died young. It was his own fault, drinking himself to death. He could not stay with being a friend of Bill's."[5]

---

[5] **A member of the Alcoholics Anonymous community (AA).** Simply put, "friend of Bill" refers to an AA member, acknowledging co-founder Bill Wilson

"Lester, I'm sorry you endured what you did as a child, but remember Louise's childhood? In comparison, yours wasn't so bad, was it?"

"Goddamn it, Gloria. You always come up with the turnaround play. Sometimes I need to bitch and vent my feelings."

"I hear you, and I feel your pain too." Gloria slid across the Caddy's big leather front seat, closer to Lester. She laid her hand on his thigh. "Right here, next to you. Isn't this better?"

"Where did the saying colder than a witch's tit come from?" she asked.

"According to Pamela, my mother the sorceress, she read it in one of the mystery novels written in the seventeenth century. Maybe she only said it was in a novel. She could have been alive then and knew firsthand ... Anyway, according to lore, witches had teats on various parts of their body to suckle their familiars or whatever. The weather was freezing cold in the witches' world, so ... use your imagination."

"Let's go with the weather. I can't imagine having multiple tits."

Lester grinned. "Might be interesting..."

"Let me call Pamela."

Lester and Gloria's drive from Miguel Gonzalez's house was silent, each dwelling on the sadness and poverty, and reliving their own memories—bereavements, troubles, accomplishments, and fortune.

CHAPTER

SEVEN

Louise was more than Lester's Gal Friday. She handled both clerical and administrative duties to ensure Lester Caine Investigations ran smoothly, requiring a minimum of Lester's attention. Louise was a native Floridian with the charm of an aging debutant, but a bite that was pure pit-bull. She had a way of sashaying across a room that drew every man's lustful eye and should be against the law.

Her father worked in the sugarcane fields when he was sober. Her mother packed up and left for California with someone she had just met, without a backward glance, never to be heard from again. Assuming the care for her younger sisters, Louise grew up fast and soon learned life's harder lessons. Despite all that, she was a charmer.

Lester often said, "*She's like a three-legged stray dog roaming the streets hunting for food and shelter. Tough, canny, surviving on grit and determination, but capable of shedding a tear. That's Louise.*"

"Lester, Lieutenant Walker is on the line." Louise purred, her sweet voice oozing through the intercom.

"Hello, Ron. I assume you're calling me about the M.E.'s report," he said.

"Yeah, finally. Meet me at the coroner's office. I want to view the body again. Since Miss Dubois hired you, there's a copy of the report for you. I'm about to leave."

"I'm on my way. ... Louise," he said as he passed her desk, "get me the weather report for the days before, after, and the day of Ruby Russell's death. Everything. Don't leave anything out."

"On it."

Lester popped his head into Gloria's office. "M.E.'s releasing his report on Ruby Russell. Get your things. We're going there now."

PALM BEACH COUNTY MORGUE
WEST PALM BEACH

The M.E.'s assistant opened the refrigerated unit. The stainless-steel table slid out, making a sound like roller skates gliding around the roller rink. A soft, blindingly white sheet draped the table, grazed the floor and concealed Russell's body. Standing across from the M.E., his assistant stood at attention, an obedient soldier waiting for his commanding officer's order. The doctor, in surgical scrubs, rubber apron and rubber gloves, nodded once, giving his adjutant his orders. Slowly, the assistant folded the sheet to her shoulders.

Everyone looking down at Ruby Russell was no stranger to death, but it still reminded them of the inevitable–their own mortality. One of them could be on that steel table, lifeless and naked, just like Ruby. Here in the morgue, the body preserved, a shield from the odor of death was unnecessary, unlike the offensive smell at homicide scenes. Some seasoned detectives placed a dab of Vicks VapoRub under their nose to disguise the rank and pungent smell of a decomposing body. Undiscovered for days, a combination of rotten meat and feces could be overwhelming. Many a cop viewing their first decomposed body had to run outside and puke. Veteran cops swear bacteria cling to nostril hair and multiply, lingering days before disappearing.

The camphor, eucalyptus and menthol combination help prevent haunting nights of the reoccurring putrid smell.

"So, Doc, tell us what we're seeing here," Lieutenant Walker questioned.

"Examining the body without a complete autopsy showed no obvious signs of trauma. There were no drugs in her blood. For that matter, only .06 blood alcohol content which translates to maybe a couple of martinis. That could cause exaggerated behavior—speaking and laughing louder than usual, impaired judgment, decreased coordination, maybe intensified emotions."

"So, no drugs, no booze to speak of. Intensified emotions ... enough to commit suicide?" Walker asked.

"Intensified emotions could go both ways. Your good moods are better and your bad moods are worse. Let me continue. There are three most common methods of suicide."

"First and most popular with women: poison or sleeping pills; second, and less common for a woman, is the gunshot; and third is hanging. More men than women die by hanging."

"But during the autopsy, I opened up her neck. I saw hemorrhaging just beneath the skin. Dozens of tiny bones in the throat were fractured. Also, the cricoid was fractured. Here, look at the X-ray. I saw spots of blood in the whites of her eyes. External pressure on the neck causes closure of the blood vessels and air passage, resulting in strangulation or, known medically, asphyxia. Asphyxia can result from one of three main categories:

1. hanging
2. ligature strangulation
3. manual strangulation.

"The type of external pressure exerted on the neck among these three entities leaves a distinctive print. Hanging results from a constricting band tightened by the gravitational pull of the body or body part's weight. A constricting band tightened by a force other than the body weight is ligature strangulation. Manual strangulation is external pressure from hands, forearms, knees or a device."

"Doc, what the hell ... Get to the point—in plain English. That jibber jabber is clear as the mud from the canals where the alligators live. Are you telling me..."

"Her intensified emotions did not have any part in Miss Russell's death," the Medical Examiner interrupted. "Yes, Lieutenant, hanging is also the safest method for killers to camouflage their crime. The presence of a fractured cricoid in a clear suicidal hanging is highly suspicious. In addition, see here? These are petechiae marks. They are tiny spots–purple, red or brown little dots, each about the size of a pinpoint, which show bleeding under the skin or in the mucous membranes."

"So, Doc, what does that tell you ... us?" Walker asked.

"There was some sort of weight, like a human knee, holding her down. Someone strangled Ruby Russell, then hung her. Her death certificate will classify her death as a homicide."

"Ah, Jesus H. Christ. Just like I said at the crime scene, Caine–a shit show." Walker muttered out loud, pacing back and forth. Then he turned to the M.E.

"Doc, look at these pictures of Miss Dubois and Mr. Chang from our initial investigation day. Caine, these copies are for you. Look at the marks on Chang's neck, hands and chest. What do you think? Could the Vic have made them while struggling and fighting for her life? Chang says they're from Lester when they were fighting."

"Go on, Lester engaged in fisticuffs?" the M.E. said sarcastically. "No, Lieutenant. Look at that mark on his neck. It's more a puncture than a scratch. It's dug in. And the three across his chest? That would be the index, middle and ring finger. They're the longest. Here, let me show you," he said. "Miss Saville, please reach across the lieutenant's chest with your hand like you are protecting yourself."

"Stop, right there. See her hand, Lieutenant? Her three fingers are identical in position to those scratch marks on Chang's chest in this photo."

"I guess you're in the clear, Caine."

"Let me see her hands and feet," Lester said.

Again, the assistant waited for his supervisor's approval. A simple nod and he exposed her hands.

"Pick up her hands and spread her fingers. Now let me see her feet."

"What are you looking for?" asked the lieutenant.

"Her toenails look like she just had a fresh pedicure. Hand me that magnifying glass. Her fingernails were cut and filed, but not by a professional. They're rough. The polish is uneven. See here and here and here. I'd bet a dollar to a donut that Ruby Russell's fingernails would not be that short or the manicure that shoddy if done by a professional. Both my ex-wives had manicures and pedicures every week. They're not cheap. Were her toes manicured when you brought her in, or done here?" Lester asked.

"We don't cut nails or remove nail polish for an autopsy. The funeral home does that when they get a body ready for viewing. She is as she came in except the coronal incision to open the cranial cavity and the incised scalp in the coronal plane behind the ear running across the vertex," said the M.E. stiffly.

"So, Ron, I know you are thinking what I'm thinking," Lester said.

"Yeah, I am. A shit show. A real shit show," Walker grumbled.

These one hundred eighty degrees turn around was not a surprise to anyone present, pointing the entire investigation in another direction ... *Homicide.*

Lester tapped on his mother's apartment door. It could compare to Edgar Allan Poe's *The Raven*, stating; "suddenly there was a tapping, as someone gently rapping, rapping at my chamber door." Lester's subconscious deliberated, saying; "boo," not to startle, but instill the thought of who it could be.

Pamela's apartment complex was nine miles between Lester's apartment and hers, measured as the crow flies. Just enough distance to fulfill the responsibilities of a dutiful son. Like the miles between, there was a distance between mother and the son who knew he was not the favored one. Pamela encouraged Lester early on to address her by her first name, *a tool*, Lester thought, *to keep her distance so she could give all the love she could give to Francis.* Francis, the golden boy, had gotten all the benefits—music, acting and dancing lessons for all the good they'd done him. His brother had been born on Saint Paddy's Day, but fate hadn't bestowed the fabled luck of the Irish on him. He'd died young.

Pamela named her favorite son after Francis of Assisi, the Italian mystic poet, canonized as a saint. She survived Francis's death by revering him. Lester sometimes wondered if Pamela believed Francis was dead. He would always remain number one in her eyes and alive in her memory. Lester often thought of a line from Shakespeare's play, *Henry IV*, spoken by Prince Henry. 'Give the devil his due.' Lester always gave his mother her due with respect.

"Really, Lester.?" Gloria rolled her eyes, stepped forward and pressed the doorbell with authority. "Now Pamela will know we're here."

The peephole swiveled, scraping along its worn-out track.

"Lester!" Pamela cried out, opening the door. "Gloria called, but it's so nice of you to visit as you so rarely do," drawing first blood. "Oh, there you are, my dear," and she gave Gloria a welcoming embrace. "I am so glad you called. Come in, come in. Lester, let me look at you. Handsome as ever, no matter how little I see of you, isn't he, Gloria?" She gave Lester an indifferent compliment and turned to Gloria.

"Yes, Pamela, he is," she answered, chalking up points for herself with Lester, knowing that was the only praise Pamela would give him.

Pamela wore her usual uniform, as Lester referred to her white fluffy slippers and pink flowered housecoat. The frock had deep pockets to keep her beloved tarot cards and Pall Mall cigarettes. She smoked Pall Malls because they were longer than other brands and she got more for her money. Besides, she believed in their slogan inside the pack. "In hoc signo vinces, by this sign shall you conquer."

Lester didn't know if his mother's ancestry included mediums or witches, but he knew not to ignore her tarot card readings. Whether she had magical powers or a connection to the supernatural, phenomena happen. Many believed in God, but Pamela maintained her own beliefs and devoutly followed the reported 1947 Roswell, New

Mexico alien landing. She also believed the cigarettes' slogan that Lester would conquer.

"Shall I make coffee? No, no, no. Let's have a drink. There must be something to celebrate. I'll get the ice. Gloria, please get the glasses. How nice! Lester, I have Jim Beam. I remember it's your favorite," Pamela said.

Between Pamela's consumption of alcohol and prescription medications, Lester never knew how he would find her. Speaking to her over the phone differed from seeing her. Like the man behind the curtain, he never really knew what was really there.

"How is Mrs. Caserta?" he asked. Pamela and her neighbor saw each other most days and Mrs. Caserta and Pamela have keys to each other's apartments. Mrs. Caserta has Lester's emergency contact–just in case.

"Oh, she's fine. I will see her tomorrow. Lester, you worry too much about me. Thank you, Gloria, I'll take three fingers. You're not like the others."

"What do you mean, Pamela?"

"You're kind and you seem to care about me. The others, Lester's two ex-wives, were doozies, particularly the French one. And Louise, as sweet as she is, is too young. Now, Lorraine, what shall I say? She told me she sits around her pool naked, reading, smoking, and drinking vodka. At least we smoke the same brand of cigarettes—Pall Malls," she chuckled.

"Pamela, that's enough. Stop with the gossip." Lester raised his voice.

"Really Pamela? She told you she sits around naked?" Gloria shot a squinty-eyed dagger at Lester. "Lester never mentioned that," she huffed. Although Gloria and Lester had no romantic commitment, Pamela's comment sparked a hint of jealousy.

"Oh, my dear. You have nothing to worry about. You have it all over every one of them."

"Thank you. Did you hear that, Lester?"

"I've got ears. Keep it up, Pamela, I can leave. Plus, you know I don't want commitment again," he muttered. "The tarot cards, NOW, or we're out of here. Please pass me my drink," Lester said, lighting a Lucky Strike.

"Light one for me too," Gloria said.

"Alright, Lester. Alright. I didn't mean ... I was only telling the truth. Do you want to shuffle, or do you want me to? Gloria, hand me my drink, please. Thank you, dear."

"You shuffle, Pamela."

"Here we go, first card. ***The Hermit Card***. A desire for solitude and self-reflection. Are you looking to take a vacation? Maybe you should consult a Buddhist priest, Lester. You work very hard. You, too, Gloria. Maybe..."

"Okay, I get it," Lester snapped. "What's next?"

"Alright, here is the ***Tower Card***. Wherever your journey takes you ... I know you'll be traveling or you wouldn't be here for a reading. Your destination will involve distraction and turmoil. I know you get into dangerous situations. Keep focused, don't stray, or let the surrounding turmoil confuse you. That can throw you off your game."

"Taking leisure isn't bringing a person to justice. Maybe we'll take a break from our work. Could self-reflection distract us if we are chasing down someone?" Gloria said. "I know we all need self-reflection."

"It could, dear. You won't know until you are in the thick of it. When and if it happens, keep your wits and remember the cards."

"Now the ***Chariot Card***. Oh, this is a good one."

"Why so good?" Gloria asked.

"You will triumph. Be victorious. You will overcome obstacles and there is conquest. So, although it trumps the ***Tower Card***, this may be after the turmoil. Don't get distracted."

"Next is **Page of Pentacles**. Oh, it's upside down."

"What does that mean? Is that bad?" Gloria eyed the card suspiciously.

"No, dear. Not at all. It simply means wasteful, illogical, bad news, rebellious young man, loss of money."

"Wow, I'm beginning to fit the puzzle pieces, Pamela. This is so incredible. I'd love to learn how to read them like you," Gloria complimented her.

"Anytime, dear."

"Next is **The Moon Card**. This has a lot of meanings. You are taking a path you are unsure of. There could be danger lurking in the dark, shown by the dog & wolf howling at the moon. You are the crawfish embarking on the path on the card. The moon's light can bring you clarity and understanding, and you should trust your intuition to guide you through this darkness."

"I always rely on my intuition, don't you, Lester? It's got us out of a lot of sticky situations," Gloria said.

"I'm very happy to hear that, dear. We have one more. This is where you told me to stop. This is number six. Shall I turn it?" Pamela asked.

"I didn't tell you to stop," Lester said. "Gloria yelled stop. Yes, turn it."

"So, the number six ... Gloria, you said stop there. Interestingly, in the Greek and Roman cultures, the number six held a place in their pantheon of gods and myths to Aphrodite and Venus, goddesses of love. It emphasized beauty, attraction and cosmic order." Pamela winked at Gloria.

"Okay, number six. The ***Knight of Swords Card*** indicates cheating in order to do harm. There you have it. Now, it's up to you to piece it all together. I'm sure you both are intelligent enough to do that."

"Now, before you go, Gloria, let me show you some of Francis's pictures and mementos from the shows where he played his accordion. Francis would have been a famous performer if he had lived."

"I remember them, Pamela. I like this one of him in his magenta silk shirt with his name down the side of the accordion," Gloria said.

"Yes, it's one of my favorites too. That was at a show Francis put on for the patients at a hospital in Yonkers. He was wonderful that way," Pamela said, sniffling and dabbing at a tear with the tissue she took from the sleeve of her housecoat.

Lester rolled his eyes. Sighing, he poured another round of three fingers for each of them.

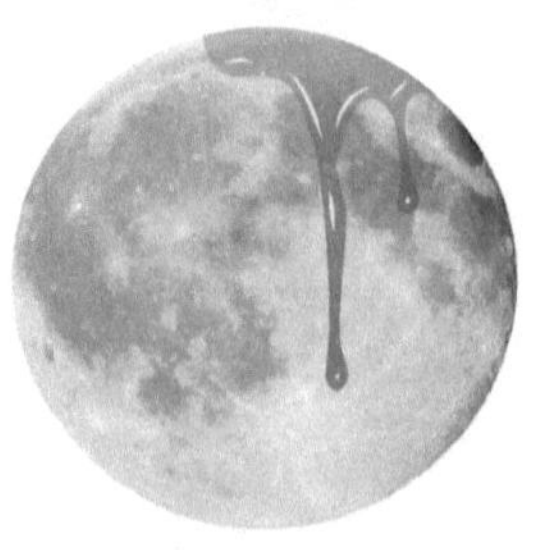

CHAPTER

NINE

DAY EIGHT
ANXIETY CREATES FEAR.

The insistent shrill of Louise's phone shattered the silence, demanding someone answer it.

"Lester Caine Investigations, this is Louise. How may I—?"

"It's Amélie Dubois. I need to speak to Mr. Caine right away." Her breathy voice, like she'd been running, halted Louise's greeting.

"Hold, please." Pressing the mute button, "Lester, it's Amélie Dubois. What do you want me to tell her?"

"I know what I'd like to tell her, but our pay day will be a big one, honey. Put her through."

"Miss Dubois ... Lester here. Calm down or I'll hang up. ... Speak nice. That's better. Now, what's the panic?"

"Mr. Caine, it's been more than a week. I've got funeral arrangements to make. Miss Russell's public is waiting. Have you read the newspapers? They're putting ideas in the minds of her fans. There's speculation the police are investigating more than Ruby's suicide because the coroner won't release the body. My phone never stops ringing. I've flown to Hollywood and back two times and met with her studio, publicist and attorneys. I'm exhausted. I haven't had a decent night's sleep since ... And when Lei and I were at the police station, they humiliated me."

"What happened?"

"I had to strip to my bra and panties in front of two female officers. They took pictures of me," she sobbed.

"Miss Dubois, I'm sorry you had to go through this. I know how difficult this must be for you, but it's SOP, standard operating procedure. Everyone has to be investigated down to their skivvies. No one will see your pictures but the police working on Miss Russell's case. I knew perps the police stripped to their birthday suit. It's a necessary evil. Maybe you should get counseling—a priest, a rabbi or a shrink."

"I have a shrink, Mr. Caine. My psychiatrist is one of Hollywood's most recognized therapists."

"I hope he or she helps you. Try to remember this difficult time is temporary. It will pass. How soon it passes depends on the complexity of the investigation." He flipped through the photos in the police file of Amélie and Chang as they spoke. *This dame is really something. A looker in her Hollywood makeup, a cute ass.*

"Mr. Caine, I'm asking for your help, please. There are millions of dollars at stake here."

"Possessions or insurance?"

"Both. I'm the Exe cutor of Ruby's will and have power of attorney. She wanted to be buried at The Hollywood Forever Cemetery in Santa Monica. She believed her spirit would go on forever when she left this earth. I can't follow her wishes until the M.E. releases her body. Why won't the Medical Examiner release her? She's not an ordinary person; she was *The Silver Screen's* Ruby Russell. And I had to stop Lei from filing assault charges against you."

"Miss Dubois—"

"Frenchie, Mr. Caine, call me Frenchie, please."

"Frenchie, the M.E. cannot release the body in an unattended, irregular death until he has enough information to issue a ruling. And people living and working inside and outside her residence complicate matters. Each person, including you, has to be cleared, and the police reach a satisfactory conclusion that agrees with the Medical Examiner. And regarding Mr. Chang. If he files charges, it's possible ... I can't say for sure ... but it's possible he could find himself on a foreign cargo ship locked in a shipping container in the middle of the Atlantic Ocean."

"Oh my God, Mr. Caine. What the hell am I into here?"

"Police work, Frenchie. Take a deep breath. Police work is not for the faint of heart. It's demanding and moves at its own pace. People don't understand and have trouble wrapping their head around it. This is real life, not the movies. We don't make snap decisions when someone's life is prematurely ended. And you're not getting into the situation. You're deeper than you know."

Frenchie gasped, a strangled sound revealing fear. Fear of what could happen to her.

"I'm trying to get a grip, Mr. Caine. I'm used to making movies, all kinds, even cop movies. But an autopsy report? She committed suicide. It's plain as day."

"To a civilian like you and the gardener. Looks can deceive," Lester said without disclosing the Medical Examiner's ruling. "Let me do the job you hired me to do."

"Can you verify everyone's whereabouts that evening, even yours and Mr. Chang's? How many people were in the house or on the grounds? Mr. Chang said there were quite a few dinner guests," Lester caught himself before he said hanging around, "that lingered. Is that correct?"

"Well, yes, sort of."

"Frenchie, Frenchie," he scolded. "That's what I mean. We must find out where everyone was, what they were doing. What the hell kind of answer is sort of? People were there or not."

"Yes, a few."

"I'm not going to play cat and mouse with you. What's a few? Two are a couple, three or more are a few. How many people, Frenchie? A few could mean twelve to fourteen. If you hold back anything, it will reflect on you. The neighbors said people were always coming and going. Have you provided Lieutenant Walker with the guest list that night? Did you tell him why they were there? Their relationship with Miss Russell? You're holding up this investigation. And he told you not to leave town without telling him. Yet you left town two times. Since you hired me, you need to tell me if you are leaving town, and where you will be if I need to contact you. I need that guest list. If you don't cooperate, the police can make it ugly for you. You don't want that. Are we clear?"

There was a long silence.

"Frenchie, I know you're still there? I hear you breathing."

"I'm here, and I'm beginning to understand. Yes, it's clear," she said. "Accepting that this is real and not a movie set where we can repeat a scene over and over is hard for me. I can't just sit around. I've lists of people to contact and things to deal with. I'll get you the guests' names and I'll keep you and the lieutenant informed if I have to leave town again."

"I'm glad we understand each other."

"Me too, Mr. Caine. I'll speak to Chang. He won't cause any problems."

Lester knew Lieutenant Walker would not release to the public that the Medical Examiner had ruled Ruby Russell's death a homicide. That meant mum's the word from his side too, especially he needed to keep Frenchie in the dark.

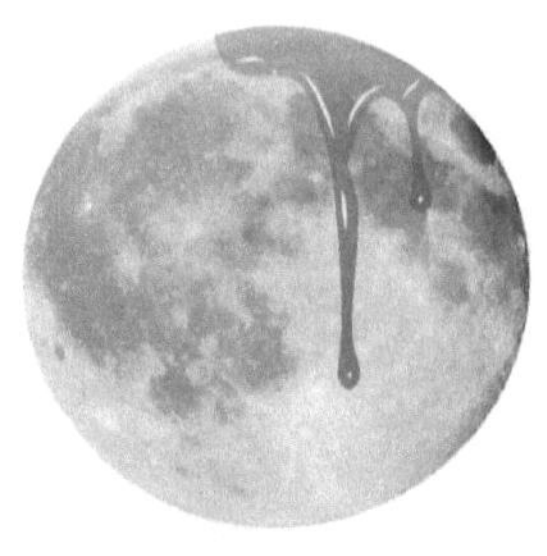

TEN

Louise put the M.E.'s report and the weather report for the day of Ruby Russell's hanging in the center of Lester's desk, where he'd immediately see it when he arrived. She made another copy for Gloria.

"Sunrise was at 6:47 a.m. The weather didn't even reach 83 degrees at the peak of the day and the humidity was 73 percent, and the M.E. says Ruby Russell died between 6 p.m. and 11 p.m. All factors considered; the environment did not speed up the decomposition. It had to be more nighttime effect in the dark. So, I lean toward the 11 p.m. hour. We got her a little after 7 a.m., so I can't dispute what the Doc says about the time of death. The night temperature was a mild 68 degrees and humidity was under fifty percent. There was a full moon. A perfect night for a murder," Lester mumbled.

"Who are you talking to? Spirits? Your Mom is good at that," Gloria said as she came into Lester's office with her copy of the reports.

"Talking to myself. Yeah, Pamela's good with the cards. Fantastic, in fact. I don't have her abilities with that shit. Sometimes I wish I did, connecting with the spirit world. I'd like to talk with my grandparents. I'm still waiting for one of them to answer me."

"Well, maybe you're not open to getting the message. Answers come in strange forms at unexpected times."

"C'mon, I want your eyes on something," Lester said.

Hmm. Gladly. Where does he want me to look? I've already seen and touched and kissed every inch of him. "I'm right behind you, Lester," Gloria said. "Louise, hold down the fort."

"You better keep in touch, Lester. You know chaos happens here when you're out of touch too long." Her eyes sent him a message. *I dream of you when you're gone. You're touching me in secret places that only make me want you more–like you must do with Lorraine and Ramona. The shit will hit the fan if it ever happens, and Gloria finds out. Oh, Lester, I'm here for you Darlin.'*

"10-4, Louise. One of us will be in touch."

"Only you Lester. Just you," Louise whispered, hand over her heart.

| THE RUBY RUSSELL MANSION

Ruby's home had been designated as an open crime scene without Amélie, Chang, or any of the domestic staff's knowledge. Investigators could come and go as they pleased, without regard to any of the household staff or residents' privacy or inconvenience.

"Lester, what the hell are we doing back here? All of Russell's staff are back in the house. Dubois hired a commercial company to clean up and straighten the forensics team's mess. You know how they leave a crime scene."

"Humor me, will you? I want to take another look."

Lester pushed the doorbell beside the front entrance. Immediately, The Ruby Waltz chimed, a melody made just for Ruby.

"Good morning," greeted the housekeeper.

"We're here..."

"I remember. Come in." She closed the massive ten-foot doors behind them. "Follow me. You can wait in the drawing room. I'll summon Miss Dubois."

"I don't understand why they call it a drawing room," Gloria said. "This room is bigger than my entire apartment."

"It's not to draw in, Miss Saville, but I can get you some pencils and crayons if you'd like," Frenchie smirked, studying Gloria.

Lester clamped a hand around Gloria's arm as she stepped toward Frenchie. He understood Gloria, but he couldn't let her beat the bitch down for that snarky comment. Frenchie didn't know she was dealing with a former Army Intelligence officer and Master Cryptologist.

"We really haven't started our day. I'm still in my pajamas. What can you possibly want now?" Frenchie asked.

Not you, twit, unless I have you in a chokehold, Gloria thought.

At that moment, the door to the drawing room swung open. Lei Chang rushed in. "What the hell! The housekeeper told me there are police here," he shouted before he recognized Lester and Gloria. "Oh, shit. It's you."

Lester flipped back his suit jacket, showing his gat on his left hip. He always wore his holster cowboy style, angling it at a twenty-degree forward slant so he could cross draw with his right hand. No one who saw that accessory could question he was a cop's cop. A visit to his office with the ribbons and medals hanging proudly on his wall would confirm it.

"Ease up, copper, I'm unarmed."

"Yeah, you'd have a helluva time concealing in that getup," Lester looked pointedly at Chang in his boxer briefs.

"I'm not going to mess with you. I'm a quick study." Chang held his hands up in surrender.

Gloria's eyes swept between Frenchie in her pajamas and Chang in his briefs. A finger pointed to one, then the other, and her internal shit-o-meter kicked up into the red zone, registering suspicion. *Are these two lovers?*

Frenchie's woman's intuition picked up Gloria's assumption.

Was it embarrassment or a guilty conscience that Gloria's darting eyes, insinuating expression, and finger gesture flushed her cheeks?

"Oh, no. No, no, no, no, no, no. It's not what you think," Frenchie blurted, waving her finger back and forth in rhythm with each denial. "Nothing like that,"

"You have no clue what I'm thinking," Gloria said.

Lester intervened, knowing Gloria was getting hot under the collar. She was poised like a wrestler about to jump from the ropes and crush her opponent. A cat fight would entertain Lester—a little hair pulling, a lot of clothes tearing, some nakedness. He'd step in and grope a little to separate them. Picturing it, he sighed. Gloria didn't fight that way.

"Get a grip," he told Gloria. Then to Frenchie, "We want to look around a little more. That's all."

"Jesus Christ. Go ahead. Do what you've got to do so I can get Ruby to her final rest," Frenchie growled. "I can't believe this. It's like a Keystone Cop movie."[6]

"We don't need a guide. You two should go back to where and what you were doing," Gloria said.

"Please send in the housekeeper," Lester said. "And I need Ruby's schedule for the past two weeks."

"I'll get everything you ask for. Give me a few minutes." Frenchie grumbled but moved to comply. She hissed as she passed Chang, "You fucking idiot. Go get dressed."

[6] Keystone Cops are fictional, humorously incompetent policemen featured in silent film slapstick Comedies

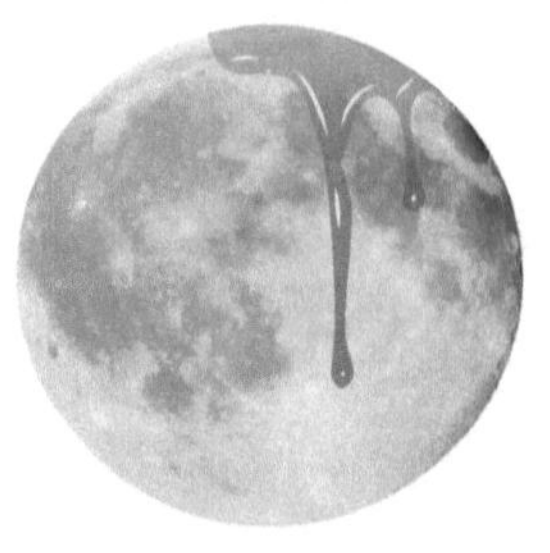

ELEVEN

| DEAD BODIES CAN TALK

"Gloria, if you look at the coroner's report, Ruby's fingernails were clipped, not filed. Remember, we looked at them at the morgue? Those were not the nails of a movie star. She had help for her domestic help. My point? She did nothing but indulge herself. Her nails should have been long with a glossy polish. Someone worked on them, but not a manicurist. Why?"

"To hide broken nails or something under them, I would say," Gloria answered.

"How about fighting for her life while she was being strangled since the M.E. has ruled her death a homicide?

I've checked with the Crime Scene Unit. They did not find any nail clippings."

"You asked to see me?" a soft voice questioned, the woman hesitating at the drawing room threshold.

"I did. I'm...."

"I know. I am a housekeeper." She waited, looking from one to the other expectantly. "You want to see me? You want a snack?"

"No snack. You cleaned up after the Crime Scene Unit left, didn't you?" Gloria asked.

"Only a little," she held her hand up, thumb and index finger extended, showing a small space between them. "Miss Dubois say a business will come. She got company from boss policeman."

"But you started right away, didn't you?" Gloria asked.

"I follow order, yes."

"Bring me the vacuum cleaner, and any other cleaning gear you used. I want to see them," Lester said.

"I bring vacuum cleaner. The rest I use just rags to wipe. I throw out. They're garbage. I get sweeper for you," she said.

"Bring newspapers too."

She mumbled something in her native language, one Lester didn't understand, and hurried from the room.

Gloria strolled to the ornately decorated teak doors.

"Jeez, Lester, you ever see doors like this? An inside door, for Christ's sake, like they wanted to barricade this room." She ran her fingers over the carving of a filmstrip and a film reel. "Ruby must've paid a mint for them. They had to be special order. That took big bucks."

The housekeeper returned, carrying the vacuum cleaner Lester had requested. Lieutenant Walker and two uniformed police officers trailed right behind her.

"Jesus H Christ, Caine. Why didn't you tell me you were coming here? And why are you here?" Walker said without a pause.

"Just checking on a few things. Remember, my clients are Ruby Russell's studio and her attorneys. I'm here for her," Lester said.

"Yeah, yeah, yeah. Let me know what those few things are. You understand?" Walker said.

"This isn't our first rodeo, Lieutenant," Gloria said. "Are you finally ruling this a crime scene?"

Walker nodded.

"Good luck with that. It's been trampled, cleaned, and re-cleaned for over a week."

"Trampled like an African elephant herd. We're here for the same reason you are, Miss Saville," Walker said.

"So, who wants to do the honors?" Walker asked, backing away from the Electrolux vacuum.

"I'll do it ... fucking men. As useful as ... " Gloria mumbled under her breath. "Do you even know how to turn one on or what to do with it?" Gloria challenged. She spread a newspaper on the floor and pulled the canister to her. She turned her head and gingerly opened the compartment, expecting a dust cloud. They'd all expected dust, dirt, and other unidentified things in the cloth bag. Lester had hoped Ruby's fingernail clippings would be inside. To their chagrin, the bag was pristine, not only empty, but new.

"Well, shit," Walker bellowed, and the housekeeper flinched. "When do you ever see a brand spanking new bag in a used vacuum cleaner?

"Miss Dubois say not keep used bag. I throw out." The housekeeper answered without meeting Walker's glare, her soft voice barely above a whisper.

"When did Miss Dubois want you to do that?" Lieutenant Walker asked in a normal tone.

She frowned, puzzled. "Long time I do this. Old bag, no more." She shrugged.

Lester turned to the housekeeper. "You said Miss Dubois told you to change the bag, correct?"

"Yes, I say that. Miss Dubois say change the bag always after we use."

"After every time you clean? Every time you use the vacuum? How often?" Gloria asked.

"Every day we vacuum. Bag goes."

"That takes care of that," Walker said glumly. "It's somewhere in the dump."

Lester, Gloria, and Walker looked at each other in disbelief.

TWELVE

| DAY 14

The door to Lester Caine Investigations slammed against the wall as if someone's life depended upon there being a lifeboat inside to escape a sinking ship. Louise pointed Edith, her .38 Smith and Wesson revolver, at the doorway. She had affectionately eponymously named her revolver Edith, as in "eat it," eat the barrel stuck in your mouth before she pulls the trigger.

"Ahhhhhhhhhhhhhhhh!" Screeching like the klaxon of a fire alarm had Lester and Gloria leaping to their feet, rushing to the door.

"You almost got your head blown off," Louise said.

"What the hell is going on here?" Gloria asked.

"Put Edith away, Louise. This is Miss Dubois, Ruby Russell's personal assistant," Lester said.

"Well, Miss Dubois, didn't your mama teach you how to enter a room?" Louise said.

"I'm sure she did, Louise. Don't you, Frenchie?" Lester referred to his introductory meeting with her and Chang the day he was called into the investigation.

Louise released the hammer on Edith. "Lucky you, this time, Miss Dubois."

"Frenchie, let's go to my office."

"I'm sorry, Lester, Gloria. I'm sorry, Louise." She called out, apologizing for her theatrics.

Louise muttered something under her breath.

It's better we didn't hear that. Lester hid a smile. He took glasses from a glass-fronted cabinet, added a bottle of Jim Beam, and poured two fingers into each glass.

"Drink this. It will calm you down." Lester's suggestion was an implied command.

"I guess it's alright even if it is still morning." Amélie's hand trembled as she lifted the glass. "Is it always like this in your office?"

"No. Sometimes it's exciting. I think I know why you're here," Lester said. "The M.E. released Miss Russell's body to the Woodlawn Funeral Home and

Cemetery in West Palm Beach this morning. Didn't Lieutenant Walker inform you? I was about to call."

"Ruby has to be buried at The Hollywood Forever Cemetery in Santa Monica. She can't stay in West Palm Beach, Lester."

"Miss Frenchie, this is Palm Beach County procedure. The Medical Examiner released her body to a funeral home. They will help you with the legal requirements to have her body taken wherever you want. You said you have a power of attorney?" Gloria said.

"Yes, Miss Saville, I do. I was going to Lieutenant Walker after you. He will tell me the same thing?"

"Yes. I'm glad we could clear up the misunderstanding. Just a communications problem," Lester said, tapping the end of his cigarette from the pack of Luckies on his lighter. "Cigarette?" he offered before touching flame to his smoke.

"No, no, thank you. I don't smoke," she answered.

"Drink up, Miss Frenchie. You'll feel more like yourself again," Gloria said, helping herself to a cigarette from Lester's pack.

"Was there anything else, Frenchie?" Lester asked.

"Yes, I have the list you asked me for. You know, the guests in the house that night..." Frenchie sobbed, interrupting her explanation. "Here it is. I must give

Lieutenant Walker the list too," she said. "I'll make Ruby's arrangements right after I finish this, this drink." Frenchie polished off her drink without flinching. "I really needed it. May I?" she said, pushing her empty glass toward Gloria.

Louise sashayed into Lester's office and approached his chair. She sniffed her disapproval at Amélie Dubois, Gloria, and Lester smoking and drinking. *Is this an office or a bar? And why wasn't I invited to the party?*

"Lester, that debacle over the vacuum cleaner's contents?" She said in a low voice.

"What about it?"

"I called the Lab. They're scraping the inside of the bag they took from their sweep. If Ruby's fingernails are in there, they'll find them."

Frenchie guzzled her drink and slammed the glass down. "I'll have another," she said.

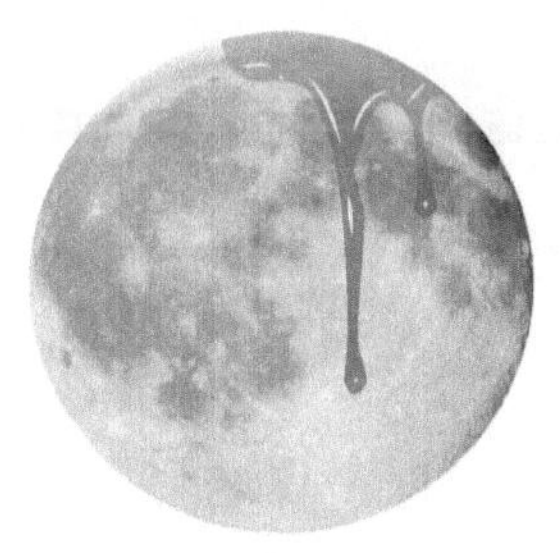

THIRTEEN

| THE LIST

Lester read the names on the guest list Frenchie gave him. She had showed who came to the mansion the night Ruby Russell died with a check mark.

Dinner Guests:

Miss Beverly Hart, Miss Russell's Palm Beach decorator

Mr. and Mrs. Bob Berman, City Councilman and wife

Mr. and Mrs. Ted Beasley, Palm Beach Mayor and wife

Amélie Dubois, Miss Russell's Assistant

Lei Chang, Bodyguard

John Arthur, Stage and Screen Actor.

Mr. Walter Thomson, Real Estate Developer

Mrs. Walter Thomson (Elizabeth), Palm Beach Divorce Attorney.

Lester picked up the phone and called Lieutenant Walker.

"Walker," his monotone, matter of fact.

"Ron, Lester here. Amélie Dubois dropped off the guest list. She is on her way to you and will give you the same list."

"I'll be here. Lester, I think we should interview them separately to see if they give the same answers," Walker said.

"I agree. The Thomsons are coming to us today. Gloria and I will start with them. I let her know the M.E. released Ruby Russell's body. I thought you called her on that."

"Didn't get to it. No rush. Miss Russell's not going anywhere. Ha! I'll tell her when she swings by with the list."

"She's going to the funeral home to arrange the transfer of the body to Hollywood Memorial. Miss Dubois will give us the details. Gloria and I are flying to Hollywood as soon as we know the funeral arrangements. Did you read the headlines?" Lester asked as he looked at the front page of the Miami Journal.

HOLLYWOOD'S BELOVED DEAD!
MEMORIAL SERVICE PENDING FOR
RUBY RUSSELL

RUBY RUSSELL, STAR OF THE SILVER SCREEN,
WILL BE LAID TO REST WHERE IT ALL BEGAN …
HOLLYWOOD.

POLICE TIGHT LIPPED WITH ONGOING
INVESTIGATION … WAS IT FOUL PLAY?
Helen Tilly

Story continued page two

Ruby Russell's Life in Section 3—ENTERTAINMENT
Helen Tilly

"I saw Tilly's headline. A real shit show here in beautiful Palm Beach where the elite meet. There will be crowds in front of Russell's mansion. I expect we'll get calls that some adventurous fan climbed the walls or gates and he's taking pictures of the balcony or trying to get inside and grab a souvenir. We'll have to assign patrol or foot patrols to control the crazies. Next, there'll be bus tours and the Island residents will complain to the Mayor that their privacy has been breached. A real freak show, Caine." He sighed deeply, running his hand through his hair.

Lester heard the all too familiar sound of the resonating dial tone breaking up Walker's litany.

There's going to be a lot of buzz in Palm Beach. Lester's thoughts raced. *Walker's not that far wrong.*

FOURTEEN

Lester Caine Investigations enjoyed proximity to The Panache Bakery, Josey's combination Pharmacy and News Stand, and Rosie's Café. As the sun began its day, regulars drawn by the aroma of freshly brewed coffee from Rosie's, the fresh cakes and pastries from the bakery, topping off their morning hustle with a stop at Josey's for the morning newspaper. Louise was a regular and could be relied on to have the morning newspaper on her desk each morning. Often, she brought tasty delights to the office from The Panache Bakery.

Louise directed Mr. and Mrs. Thomson to the conference room and served coffee, her southern manner sweeter than two lumps of sugar. Louise was no hot house delicate flower when circumstances called for toughness. She introduced Mr. and Mrs. Thomson and left them with Lester and Gloria. Then she closed the door, returning to the morning newspaper.

"What the hell is this all about, Caine?" Mr. Thomson growled. The first words out of his mouth revealed his agitation.

Lester restrained from using cop interrogation tactics, like getting two inches from Thomson's face while answering him, or using threats, coercion, provocation, good cop-bad cop, or separating him and his wife.

"Good morning, to you, Mr. Thomson," Lester smiled, enjoying himself.

"Easy Dear," Mrs. Thomson said, patting his arm. "My husband is uncomfortable when he's questioned about close friends. He feels it's disloyal to talk about them. We're all on the same page. Ruby was our dear friend, Mr. Caine. I'm sure you understand, Miss Saville.

"I understand, Mrs. Thomson. My father had a temper. You know, Italian culture, head of the house thing," Gloria added.

"I'm not like that," Mr. Thomson said, slapping the table with the palm of his hand.

His reaction to her allusion of his temper was what Gloria wanted to see. And he fell for it. His wife squirmed in her chair. She reached for his hand and squeezed it, a gesture to shut the fuck up. If she hadn't, it's probable he would have said and done much more.

"I'm an attorney, a divorce attorney. I'm not familiar with criminal law. We all know what involvement in an unsavory situation can do to reputations, don't we? It's crazy to think anyone could murder Ruby. Everyone loved her."

"Not everyone, Mrs. Thomson. No one is universally loved. Surely you've run into that in your profession," Gloria said.

"After the first newspaper story, everyone's calling foul. That can't be true ... is it?" Mrs. Thomson silently pleaded with Lester to deny the allegations.

"That's what we'd like to find out," Lester said.

"We're here voluntarily and we're meeting with the Police Lieutenant. How can we help, Mr. Caine?" Mrs. Thomson said.

"Why don't you start by telling us how you know Miss Russell?" Gloria asked.

"I handled Miss Russell's divorce, and we became friends."

"Miss Dubois never mentioned Miss Russell had been married or divorced," Lester said.

"Tell us about her divorce," Gloria suggested, appealing to her woman-to-woman.

"Well, it was simple. One of my easiest cases. There were no children. It was amicable. No drama," she said.

"And her husband?" Lester asked.

"He's an actor."

"John was at the dinner party," Mr. Thomson volunteered.

"That's right. They parted as friends. We all became close during the proceedings. It just happened. Each was wealthy, so there were no alimony disputes or squabbles over splitting property." She looked at Lester with the suggestion of a smile while her bare foot slipped under the cuff of his trousers and crawled up and down his shin as she spoke.

"That would be John Arthur?" Lester asked, glancing at the dinner guest list.

"John, Mr. Arthur, was a hitter for the other team. Ruby and John's marriage was a lavender marriage, one of convenience, a show for the press and their public. They were each other's beards. According to Ruby, the marriage was never consummated. Mr. Arthur didn't confirm it, but I didn't ask. You know how that goes. We worked closely with her studio and their attorneys so the press would believe the marriage and subsequent divorce were real. Actually, the hush-hush was more for John's sake. You know, leading man and action film roles. The coverup was a studio decision. When you're under contract, Mr. Caine ... Lester, the studio owns you. What the studio says goes."

Mrs. Thomson was forthcoming without incriminating. She knew how to turn a phrase to her advantage. It had served her well, financially and personally. Her intellect and poise had earned her hundreds of thousands of dollars.

"What she said," Mr. Thomson nodded, leaning toward his wife. "We all became friends during the divorce. Can we move on ... please?"

"If I understand you, they were not friends with benefits. No fear one would disclose the other's secrets, no financial squabbles. Never heard of that much cooperation in a divorce," Lester said, thinking of his two strikes.

"How about professional jealousy?" Gloria asked.

"There were no signs their friendship had changed, Miss Saville." Mrs. Thomson answered, a coy smile directed at Lester.

Lester flashed a smile, acknowledging her interest.

"Who is Miss Russell's beneficiary since she had no children? Any siblings?" Lester asked.

"I'm not a probate attorney ... Lester. No, Ruby didn't have siblings. Her parents–both dead. My guess would be Frenchie, I mean Amélie, Miss Dubois. They were like sisters," Mrs. Thomson said. "Maybe some charitable bequests."

"Can we go now? We really don't know anything else," Mr. Thomson said.

"Almost, Mr. Thomson. Tell us what you do," Lester asked, turning to him.

"What do I do?"

"How do you make your living?"

"What does that have to do with Ruby Russell?"

"My husband is a real estate developer. Go on, darling, tell him," Mrs. Thomson looked at him out of eyes that shouted, *just answer the fucking questions so we can get out of here.*

"I get people together, use their money to buy and sell land. Some properties we develop into commercial stores and office buildings," he said. "Some we hold until the price is right. Then, we sell."

"Was Miss Russell one of your investors?" Gloria asked.

"Yes, and no. She was until she decided she didn't want in the game anymore," Mr. Thomson said.

"Did that upset you ... a cash cow that stopped giving milk?" Lester asked. Taking a pack of Luckies from his pocket, he offered each one of them a smoke. Then he tapped and lit his.

"I'll take one," Mr. Thomson said.

"None for me, thank you," Mrs. Thomson replied. "Mr. Caine, my husband has other investors. Miss Russell was one of many. Her ex-husband was an investor too. The last development, a hotel in Miami, was ... complicated. Miss Russell could not afford to be linked with projects featured in the tabloids."

"She pulled out. That's it, nothing more," Mr. Thomson added.

"What complications exactly?" Gloria asked.

"Delivery delays, trade unions, code inspections, city officials., cost overruns. Everyone had a hand out, expected *bonuses*, if you know what I mean. You must know who and what I'm speaking of. One of them lives on Palm Island," Mr. Thomson said.

Al Capone, the Chicago gangster, lived on Palm Island, Lester and Gloria knew, as did the local authorities and the world. Mr. Capone managed his extensive criminal empire through a network of appendages, aka his lieutenants. They bribed politicians, law enforcement, and government officials to minimize or eliminate interference in his business. Capone heavily invested in the Miami community.

"So, Mr. Thomson, you know our mutual friend on Palm Island?" Lester asked.

"Can I offer either of you a drink?" Gloria asked, hoping to loosen them up.

"No," both answered almost in unison.

"I never met the man and never wanted to. He has his people who know people who know me. That's how it goes. Caine, you have the guest list. Connect the dots. Those two individuals came to me when we were putting the hotel together. If we didn't bring in outside investors besides Ruby and John, the project would have gone south, a lot further south than Miami. Those two, who they were, got us who we needed to get a stamp of approval to complete the hotel. That's how it works—one person to another, to a third, then another, and so on. That way, no individual can be implicated in any wrongdoing. C'mon, Caine, you know the score. You've been around the block–a lieutenant with the NYPD. I bet you even broke bread or had a drink with a few movers and shakers," Mr. Thomson said.

Lester shot a look at Gloria. Their acquaintance, Freddy Two Fingers, had helped them track down the Nazi War Criminal the previous year.

"I did not expect the project to be so difficult," Thomson continued. "We barely broke even. Ruby was under pressure during this investment, her divorce and all it involved. The studio demanded she separate herself from these investments, even hired a public relations firm to quash the rag papers," Mr. Thomson said.

"But Mrs. Thomson said it was a simple divorce, possibly the easiest, most amicable one she handled. Isn't that right, Mrs. Thomson?" Gloria stated.

"What are you asking?" Mrs. Thomson asked, narrowing her eyes at Gloria.

"Just clarifying. We just want to know who was with Miss Russell the last night of her life and their connection to her," Lester said.

"Yes, Miss Saville, the divorce was simple and uncomplicated. However, nothing was really simple or wholly private with Ruby's status. The studio made demands on her for public appearances and interviews. The press hounded her about her divorce and the Miami hotel, trying to connect her to Capone. Photographers snapped her photo everywhere she went. Her film shooting schedule was grueling, sometimes running fourteen hours a day. Her lifestyle allowed very little time to recharge, to sleep. It wore on her," Mrs. Thomson said in her best courtroom demeanor.

"What time did you leave?" Gloria asked.

"We all pretty much left together, wouldn't you say, dear?" Mrs. Thomson looked at her husband for confirmation.

"Yes, I would." He said.

"Well, what time was it?" Gloria asked.

"About nine-ish." Mrs. Thomson mumbled.

"Yes, that's correct," Mr. Thomson agreed.

"And everyone, you said; 'all pretty much left together.' All of you drove private cars? Or did you have a limo transport everyone? You would have had to be one of the last out the door to see that 'all pretty much left together,'" Gloria said, dwelling on the guests' departure.

"We're out of here," Mr. Thomson said, seething. "Let's go dear. We have to meet up with that Walker cop,"

"You have my number, Mr. Caine. If there is anything else?" Mrs. Thomson said.

Lester muttered, "Yeah, I got your number, all right."

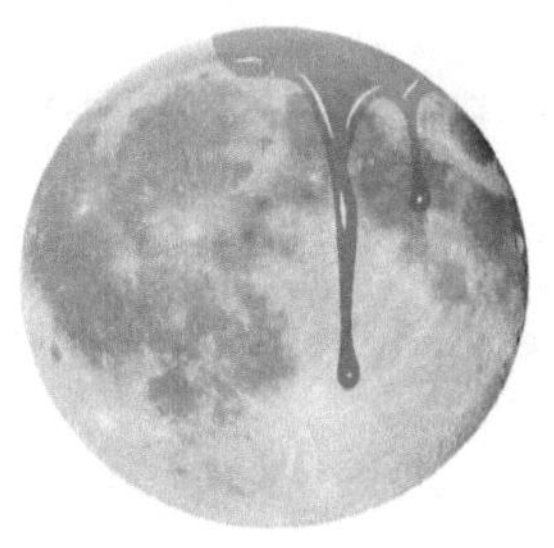

FIFTEEN

| DAY 18

Louise called the after-hours answering service every morning after she set up the coffee.

"Lester, Miss Dubois left a message. They're taking Miss Russell's body to Hollywood and funeral arrangements are pending.

"Did she leave a number?"

"Yes. I have it here," she said, walking into Lester's office, handing him the phone message with one hand and his coffee, black, with the other. She sat herself familiarly on the corner of his desk in her usual fashion, showing off legs that were like Radio City Music Hall Rockette dancers. Her legs could easily help her seek fortune and fame on Broadway with its glitter, glitz and hopeful dreams—something Louise knew nothing about. She was a hometown girl, never out of the state, much less New York. Most young Florida girls didn't aspire beyond a man, marriage, and kids.

If she lifts her skirt any higher, her gynecologist and I can compare notes ... strictly professional. Oh yeah! She leaned in, straightened his tie, treating him to a view of her breasts down the neckline of her loosely fitted blouse. His imported Taylor of Old Bond Street Cologne from London just tempted her to misbehave. Lester knew his place and kept it. He expected Louise's attempt to get him to relax his scruples.

"Okay, okay. Morning, Louise. Let's get down to business, starting with moving your derriere off the desk."

Louise always hoped it meant the business she wanted with Lester—getting naked. She didn't care about the twelve-year difference in their ages. To her disappointment, it never turned out how she wished it. She knew he bedded Lorraine Vanderbilt, the widow of the judge whose murder he'd help solve, and Ramona from Lola's Jazz Club. Louise knew, but Gloria didn't, and she was his main squeeze. Louise would settle for any position in his lineup.

"Miss Dubois said she'll be around if you need her. After tomorrow, you can reach her at Abracadabra Studios. The number is right there."

"Abracadabra didn't work in Ruby's favor," Lester mumbled. "Abracadabra. You know, used after incantations or sleight of hand in magic shows," Lester answered.

"What are you saying, Lester? I don't know what you mean."

"Abracadabra. Used to ward off misfortune, harm, or illness in some magical form. Magicians use it in their act, waving their so-called magic wand and saying, 'Abracadabra.' Then something successfully appears or disappears or changes to something else."

"Well, sure as shit, Abracadabra didn't work for poor Ruby Russell." Louise stated as a matter of fact.

"No, Louise, it didn't. Let's get the day started. Get me Lieutenant Walker on the phone."

"Lieutenant Walker, how can I help you?"

"Ron, It's Lester."

"I'm listening, Lester. You must have something, or you would not be calling me this early unless it's for that steak dinner you owe me."

"How could I forget? You remind me every day. I've got you covered. We've interviewed the dinner guest list, and everyone says the same thing. They left *en masse* about nine o'clock, except Miss Dubois and Mr. Chang, who apparently live there. So, they were there all night."

"I got the same bullshit stories. Sounded too pat, almost rehearsed. Besides, I've got to believe the Mayor and the City Councilman in their positions."

"Ron, don't be so naïve. You know as well as I the power of those positions, what they can do and cannot do," Lester said.

"Are you saying something about them?"

"No, but your cop sense knows as well as I do everyone is under suspicion until they're not." Lester would not reveal all the minutiae from his interview with the Thomsons.

"And can you believe that about Ruby Russell and John Arthur? Do you believe Russell was his beard? If that ever gets out, how many women's hearts will break, including my wife's? I'll let her have her fantasy and never tell her. He was and still is a leading man."

"Yeah, you're right. Russell's studio, I suppose like all the studios, had their formula for successful hits. Many of them are hooked on war and hero films since we won. Warner Brothers did crime films while Russell's studio, Abracadabra, did melodramas and romance with her leading man, John Arthur, and swashbucklers with Errol Flynn or Clark Gable that brought it acclaim. Box office hits one after another," Lester said.

"You know what this is sounding like to me, don't you, Lester?" Ron said.

"I do, Ron, I do," Lester answered. "A rehearsed dialogue among the dinner guests. Where I'm not connecting the dots is with all the guests unless..."

"Unless what, Lester?"

"Ah, nothing, just thinking out loud. So, when are you going to release the findings that it's a homicide?"

"You're the one getting the big payday. I'm giving you the go ahead. Tell her. The newspapers will get it the day after tomorrow. You're a big boy, Lester. I'm sure you've delivered that message hundreds of times. Good luck."

"I'll call you." Lester said and hung up the phone.

"Gloria, get in here," Lester yelled across the office, tapping his pack of Lucky Strikes to ease one out.

"Jesus, Lester, we have an intercom," Gloria retorted. "Before you say anything, I checked the local hardware stores. Thankfully, there are only a half dozen from here to Boynton Beach going south and north to Lake Worth, where your mother lives.”

“Speaking of, I’ve got to go see Pamela,” Lester said.

“I find it interesting you call your mom by her first name. Anyway, I found out that our friend, Mr. Chang, bought some items at Alvi’s Paint and Hardware store here in West Palm.”

“Oh, yeah? I’ve been there once or twice. Their wooden floors may be rickety and uneven, but they know their stuff. My god, rows of bins of whatever you need.”

“My father would come up from Miami to go there. He said, ‘If a hardware store doesn’t sell nails scooped out of a bin and weighed on a scale, it’s not a real hardware store. The clerks know exactly every nut, bolt, and screw size you need and where it’s located. They can take you right to it and give you advice on anything for any project. It’s worth the ride up. Besides, I get your mother out of the house.’ It’s a nice mom and pop store. Al and his wife Marcia have been there for years.”

“And...”

“Oh, I got lost there for a moment. They remember a Chinese man who fit the description of our Mr. Chang purchasing rope, industrial tape, shovel and two nuts and bolts, which were different sizes. I spoke with Big Al directly, who remembers a Chinese guy. Big Al said it was odd. The guy walked around the store, randomly picking up things. No list or drawings of what he was working on. It was like he really didn't know what he wanted to buy. He kept looking out the front window at a parked car in front. Big Al remembered the car, a Lincoln Continental convertible, a woman in the driver's seat. I asked what she looked like. He wasn't any help there. He was more interested in the car. It reminded him of the cars he sees along the highway with an ocean view where the woman's head scarf blows behind her like a flag in the breeze. The last thing Chang asked was if they sold stethoscopes. I sent my report to Walker. He said he'd give it to the D.A."

Lester howled with laughter. "A stethoscope? Don't tell me. They sell those, too? I guess he wanted to be sure Ruby wasn't breathing. Good work, Gloria."

"What was so important, Lester?"

"Walker just asked me to deliver the news to Miss Dubois. I think you should come."

"Alright, but you're the one who has to tell her."

"Louise, call Amélie Dubois and tell her we're on our way. We have important news."

"Maybe we should have a drink first. We may need it," Lester said, opening the cabinet.

The melodic sound of the Ruby Waltz rang when Gloria pressed the doorbell.

"Miss Dubois is expecting you in the drawing room," said the housekeeper.

"Mr. Caine, Miss Saville, what is so important? I'm inundated with...." She sighed.

"Perhaps you'd like to sit," Gloria said.

"Okay, I'm sitting."

"Where is Mr. Chang?" Lester asked.

"He had personal business to take care of and took off for Hollywood before I could go."

"Do you know where he can be reached?" Gloria asked.

"I have it somewhere. So, tell me, please. Why are you here?"

"Miss Dubois," Gloria said, hesitating, turning to Lester.

"Amélie, we're here because Ruby Russell's death is now a homicide," Lester quickly said.

She slid off the sofa onto the floor, fainting.

"Ah, shit," Lester mumbled.

"What'd you expect?" Eyes wide, hand spread across her chest, Gloria mimed. "Oh, my goodness. Let's have some fucking tea."

"That about sums it up," Lester said.

CHAPTER

SIXTEEN

| LOLA'S JAZZ CLUB.

Lester wanted to relax before heading to Los Angeles for Ruby's funeral. That scene was inevitable. Lola's was a hot Palm Beach night spot that drew crowds every night, and it was Lester's favorite watering hole. Claudette welcomed Lester on stage to blow notes from his beloved 1940 French Besson Brevete trumpet. He affectionately named his trumpet for Calliope, the Greek Goddess who prevailed over poetry. Regulars at Lola's knew they were in for a treat when Lester joined the ensemble.

Bourbon was another catharsis for Lester. Ramona, his favorite barkeep and sometime lover, completed his decompression routine ... away from cop business and away from Gloria. There was never a dull moment at Lola's or with Ramona. He never knew what to expect.

A huge horseshoe-shaped bar kept four barkeeps busy. Their uniform tuxedo trousers and starched white shirt and tie identified them. Ramona watched for Lester, knew he would sit in his usual corner spot in her section of the bar, and set a glass with two fingers of bourbon there. They could cozy up in conversation in between Ramona's drawing drinks, serving them, and playing her trivia game for money with the customers in her section. Each answer she or her counterpart, Carl, answered correctly, put two bucks into the jar on the bar, excluding tips. If they were incorrect or stumped— after consulting the trivia encyclopedia Ramona kept at the ready—the customer got a free round of drinks. It was a mainstay of Lola's. The patrons ate it up, crowding the bar.

"Ah, Lester. So good to see my very own Dick Tracy," she whispered in his ear, leaning across the bar to greet him with a kiss. "I've missed you."

Lester loved hearing he was her own Dick Tracy, the Sunday comic strip character. Tracy was an intelligent detective with an underlying code of "crime doesn't pay," who solved crimes using tough and often violent law enforcement.

Oohs, ahhs, and wolf whistles circled the bar, stirring Ramona to turn and raise her hand over her head, giving everyone the digitus impudicus gesture which translated to the offensive fuck you finger, initiating back slapping and laughter.

"Ramona, I'm here for you. Don't pay any attention. Most of them are on a bender," Lester said.

"I don't mind sharing you with Calliope," she said. *And whoever else is in your little black book.*

"See, Ramona, you understand me."

"And I understand what you and I want out of whatever you call this," she said, pointing her finger back and forth between the two of them. "I'm good with it."

Lola's regular quintet, *Midnight Train,* was one of the best musical jazz groups in Palm Beach. They had been featured in *Jukebox, Down Beat,* and *Society Rag.* When they started vamping for their next set of the night, the crown settled down. Lester scheduled his arrival right before the second set when the crowd was calm, dinner finished, plates and silverware didn't rattle, and waiters served Lola's famous dessert, Torta Barozzi.[7] The night was young; and the crowd was ready to imbibe and beguiled by the beauty and eroticism of Claudette Moreau. Her name was fitting, its meaning often associated with grace, elegance, and sophistication. Moreau meant dark-skinned, fitting for the French Créole beauty. Claudette's voice, in pitch and timbre, invited your heart into hers. You became one. She was a femme fatale. Lester knew firsthand, having had a now and then affair with her until she married Dino, the drummer.

Lester reached for his pack of Luckies. Before he could get a cigarette out, Ramona held her lighter for Lester to lean in and light up. All the bar keeps did it for Lola's customers as a rule of thumb, but Ramona lighting Lester's smoke meant something more than service. It was symbolic for him to *put out my fire*. Lester wrapped his hands around her hand, eyes locking in a shared moment.

---

[7] Torta Barozzi-Known as "black cake." A sinfully delicious dense dark chocolate, flourless confection, flavored with coffee, chopped peanuts, and almonds.

Ramona knew at this point the night was hers. Playing cops and robbers with handcuffs was in the cards.

Lester glanced down to the other end of the bar, meeting eyes with the guy staring at him and Ramona. This wasn't one of those stares where the person looked quickly away once you caught him looking. No! This person didn't break contact. He wanted them to feel his glare, to make them uncomfortable. Lester's detective antenna kicked in, picking up what he called *The Fruit of the Poisonous Tree*–a real dick vibe. He studied the sleazy looking guy with a pencil-thin mustache, one worn by guys who bought their rubbers from a vending machine in the men's room at a gas station.

"Ramona, you still carry the gift I gave you?"

"Sure do, Lester. Locked and loaded with the dumdums you gave me." She tapped her right pocket, felt the .25 Barretta Lester gave her as a Christmas gift.

"Good. Those hollow point bullets mushroom on impact, making a hole a grave digger wouldn't be able to fill."

"No worries. I spotted him a while ago. You taught me well. I was waiting for him to make his way to my side of the bar. I doubt he will now that you're here and he saw how we are with one another. I'm glad about that."

Midnight Train and Claudette's soulful melodies set the mood for the evening and what was to follow. Claudette always noticed Lester. His aura radiated a distinctive sexual presence and a masculinity that attracted women. She finished her second forty-five-minute set, made eye contact with Lester at the bar, and nodded to him. That signaled Lester and Calliope to join her and the ensemble on stage, the moment he had waited for. Ramona filled his glass. He removed his jacket, loosened his tie, rolled up his sleeves, and made his way to the stage, Calliope in one hand, his Jim Beam in the other.

Each note Lester blew was poetry—smooth, rich, soft, luscious, silky, and velvety. He knew what blowing sweet notes and being on stage did for him and its effect on the audience and at the bar. The same rush the New York Broadway actors referred to as the roar of the crowd and the smell of the greasepaint used as make-up. Each gave them a thrill on and off stage, just like playing with Midnight Train did for Lester with Calliope. He had played with the best of them when he lived in New York, frequenting the haunts of all the great clubs that lined 52nd Street, Swing Street, the east side jazz clubs, with the likes of Billie Holiday, Chick Webb, Coleman Hawkins, and Thelonious Monk. Each smooth note Lester blew sailed over the heads of the one-hundred fifty jazz aficionados that filled Lola's smoke-filled dining room. His notes were like pristine clouds, sailing overhead, placing each one of them in your mind, in your heart, invoking gladness, sadness, memories, scarring your soul, every part of your being.

This was Lester's time. He had the best of both worlds–on stage with Calliope and Ramona to top off the end of the night, or more accurately, the wee hours of the morning. In between his soulful notes, Lester sang for the first time, a song of a broken heart, not caring how he sounded.

It had to be you,

It had to be you

I wondered around, finally found somebody who

Could make me be true, could make me be blue

And even be glad just to be sad

Thinking of you

Some others I've seen

Might never be mean, might never be cross

Or tried to be boss, but they wouldn't do

'Cause nobody else gave me a thrill

With all your faults I love you still

It had to be you, crazy old you,
It had to be you.[8]

Heads turned. This was a different Lester. Patrons of the club were used to Lester and Calliope, but they had never heard his voice, never heard his alter ego before. This was an aphrodisiac for Ramona and many of the fillies in the audience, married or not. For Lester, this was the roar of the crowd and his smell of the greasepaint.

Mustache Pete made his way to Ramona's section, sitting where Lester had been. Much to Ramona's chagrin but not surprise, he made his move like a sneak thief after Lester left for the stage.

"That spot is spoken for," Ramona said, looking him in the eye.

"Not while he's on-stage, making love to that horn and belting out a song. He's damn good for a flatfoot." He said.

Ramona's mind raced. *How does he know Lester was or is a private eye?*

"What are you talking about?"

---

[8] It Had To Be You is a popular song composed by Isham Jones, with lyrics by Gus Kahn.

"You know, what he was and what he is now—a private dick."

"I don't get you, mister."

"You will, sweetheart," he said.

"I'm not your sweetheart. Do you want me to pour you a drink?" *Maybe I could drop some rat poison in it.*

"I'd like that and stir it with your finger."

She poured it, then staring him in the eye, stuck her finger in and stirred it like he asked.

"See, tastes better with your touch. I imagine everything, and I mean everything, is better with your touch."

"Believe me, it does, and that's something you'll never know. It's in your best interest to finish your drink and leave. On the house," she said.

"Maybe," tilting his head, he raised his eyebrows with a gesture that said, I'll think about it.

"Don't think too long. If I hit this button, your ass is grass," Ramona threatened.

"No need. I've seen the goons ... uh, security buttoned up tight in their tailored suits. I'll finish and be on my way. See you around, sweetheart." He gulped the last of his drink and got up to leave.

Closing was a process. The U.S. government had implemented a closing time for all bars at two a.m. When Ramona rang the bell for last call, everyone had to tally up, put in orders to satisfy the next round the dissolutes would want. Tonight, Lester hung around the stage playing riffs with several musicians while Ramona took care of business, finally finishing about three a.m.

They left together, Lester walking Ramona to her car, then back to his to follow her home. She lived in a hidden gem, Northwood Hills. The street layout was unique, a figure-eight with the highest natural peaks in South Florida at 44 feet above sea level. Northwood Hills was a short distance from Lola's and once was inhabited by rum runners. Ramona drove because of her wee morning hours and she lived alone.

She pulled into her parking space before her apartment. Lester noticed someone sitting in a car a few doors down. He smelled cigarette smoke and saw the lit ash. Cutting his headlights, he coasted to a stop, stealthily getting out. With no noise, the man got out of his car and jogged toward Ramona. Lester pulled his revolver, ran toward them, yelling; "Ramona, run!"

The man faced Lester, a gun in his hand. Lester shot off two rounds—BLAM! BLAM!

His .38 hollow point bullets whizzed at 690 feet per second, hitting like a loud slap. The man dropped. Ramona heard the shots. Her breath caught. She was safe in her apartment, dialing the police. She peered outside, but she couldn't see beyond the curb in the dark. Stepping out, she saw a body lying in the street where he'd fallen. The smell of burning gunpowder wafted through the silent night. She drew her Baretta, wary, until the dim streetlight showed her it wasn't Lester. She saw blood pool around the body on the ground. An ambulance wouldn't help him. He didn't stand a chance.

"Lester? Thank God you're alright. You are alright, aren't you?" She hugged him tight.

"I'm good," he said. "Help me. Take my hankie. I'll roll him enough for you to reach his wallet. Use the hankie. Hurry while I hold him. Find his driver's license and read his name and address to me."

"He doesn't have a wallet. Do you know this guy?"

"I don't recognize him. No ID? That's a professional's MO. They don't carry any for this reason. If the tides turn and they wind up where he is. I'm sorry, Ramona, sorry you got caught in the middle of whatever this is."

Lester put two smokes in his mouth, lit them, and gave one to Ramona. He knew what came next.

"Put your gun away. Don't mention you have one." Lester rallied.

The wailing sirens and glaring strobe lights on the police car woke the neighborhood. None other than Lieutenant Walker stepped out.

The neighborhood lit up like a Broadway show. Porch lights came on one after another and people ran out in their bathrobes, slippers and pajamas flooding the street and onto their porches.

"Jesus H Christ. You've got to be kidding me. Of all the people in all the world! You? I would never have expected you, Lester. Oh, I'll take that back," he said. "Ever think we could just meet over a cup of joe, maybe shoot the breeze without a body? What's the story, Caine?" Walker asked, blowing out a heavy sigh. He walked the scene, mumbling to himself, occasionally shaking his head.

"Lieutenant, good to see you too." Lester's response was quick, to the point, and sarcastic.

"God damn it. It's almost 4 a.m. Don't you ever sleep? It's a good thing I can see this stalwart citizen's gun in his hand, Caine. The stars are with you on this one. You know the drill. Give me your gun and your P.I. license." He held out his hand and passed them to a uniformed officer. "Bag it and tag it," he said. "Secure the scene. Get all these people back... NOW!"

"Who called this in?" Walker asked.

"I did," Ramona answered.

"Who are you? What are you doing here? Do you know this guy?" pointing to Lester.

"Yes, I know him. Lester, I mean. I live here. Right there," pointing. "My name is Ramona."

"Does Ramona have a last name?" Walker asked like a dentist ready to pull a tooth, and the patient didn't want to say which one to pull. The uniformed patrolman stood by while Walker wrote the details.

"So, help me understand, Caine. You and Ramona here were about to have a nightcap. Instead, you capped this guy. Do you know him? Why did this happen?" Walker asked without taking a breath.

"Shit. Another long night here and at the station, Caine. You too, Ramona. The M.E. should be here sometime soon. We know about that, don't we, Caine?" Walker sighed deeply.

"No, answering your question, I don't recognize him. Maybe a stick-up for my wallet."

"What about you, honey?" Walker asked Ramona.

"Never saw him before," she replied.

"This patrolman will take you to the station," Walker said.

Lester and Ramona hoped they would find out who was lying there with two holes in his chest.

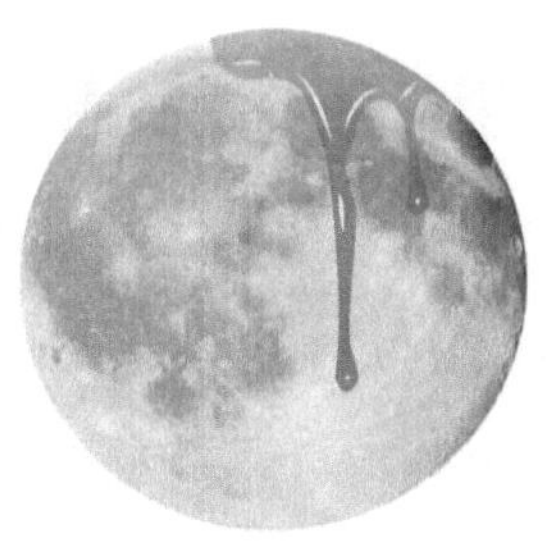

CHAPTER

SEVENTEEN

| GOOD NEWS IS GOOD.

"Lester, Lieutenant Walker called. You can pick up your gun and license at headquarters. You are in the clear," Louise said. "Walker said they all should be so clean and easy. Only you could pull that off. He asked if you were born on St. Patrick's Day. You know what they say, 'the luck of the Irish' and all that rot. You're not Irish, but your brother, Francis, was born on St. Paddy's Day. They haven't ID'd the dead man yet, and they're still waiting to run him for any priors. Your things will be at the front desk waiting," Louise said, drying her tears with a tissue.

"Oh, and Lester? Based on the M.E.'s report, the District Attorney issued an arrest warrant for Lei Chang for the murder of Ruby Russell. The marks on Chang's body and the rope purchase are further evidence."

"Wait 'til the papers get hold of that. ... Uh, Louise, are you okay?" Lester asked.

"I'm good. I'm glad you're not hurt or dead, that's all."

Lester knew it was more than that. Something must have triggered emotions from her buried childhood memories. Louise was careful not to let her moods show on the job. She let nothing interfere with her work. She had excellent research skills, and Lester thought she had the making of a competent P.I..

"What are you going to tell Gloria about last night?" she asked, surprising him.

Lester looked at his wristwatch. Gloria would arrive soon. Chances were, she hadn't heard of last night's incident. He hadn't formed an explanation. Hadn't thought he needed one. If she asked, he'd tell her he was blowing notes at Lola's Jazz Club and Lola talked to him about one of the female barkeeps who felt threatened by a sleazy guy. The guy's attentions possibly had crossed over into stalker territory. She asked him to escort the female barkeep home. End of story.

It wasn't a secret that Lester jammed with the musicians at Lola's Jazz Club. He considered the club his second home. Gloria might have suspicions, but so what? She had never asked him about it.

Detective Walker's bellowing voice registered several decibels over the squad room conversation and the police radio chatter. Lester followed the echoes to the lieutenant's corner office. What was supposed to be waiting for him at the front desk Walker held.

"Okay, Ron, I'm here. Let's get it over with. Chew me up and spit me out. I've got nothing to add, and nothing to hide," Lester said.

"I've nothing to beat you with, Lester. It was a justified shooting. Here's your gun and license." He pushed it toward him. "I convinced the D.A. to issue an arrest warrant for Chang."

"Louise told me. All the evidence points to him, but what's his motive?" Lester pondered aloud.

"Caine, this is crazy. In all my years, I've never had to deal with the public or all the officials like the Russell case. I've heard from the top—the Governor's office and the Attorney General. At least we got something solid, Lester. Thank God we got photographs of those measly scratch marks and that small puncture wound on Chang. The rope your gal discovered he bought at the hardware store? That was solid work. The D.A. was waiting for a direct link to Chang personally to Ruby's murder. The rope clinched it for him. I hate to say this, but I'm counting on you and so are Russell's fans to find this bastard."

"Gloria and I are heading out to Hollywood for Ruby's funeral. For all we know, he may be there. Let's hope he's unaware there's an APB out for him. I'll take a copy of his arrest warrant with me. We'll sniff around and see what we find," Lester said.

"Well, maybe you can dig deep and use some dirt from Ruby's grave. You know, get some dirt on somebody who knows his whereabouts. You better get some bigger shovels, 'cause mine aren't working. I don't even know where to look for him. For all we know, he's back in China. I've contacted Interpol and the Los Angeles Police. They're aware he's wanted. He's considered armed and dangerous."

From his days as an NYPD homicide detective, Lester was no stranger to all the bullshit paperwork he just finished. In his opinion, all that paper was a time waster, although a necessary evil.

He drove by the Palm Beach County Appraiser's office on his way back to the office and swung into public parking. He'd been meaning to look up some information for a while. Then he called Gloria.

"Gloria, get Louise and meet me out in Belle Glade." He rattled off an address on the edge of the Everglades.

"What's—"

"Don't ask and don't tell Louise," Lester interrupted.

"But Lester..." *Dammit, this is unlike him, giving me a cryptic message with not a hint of what it's about.*

"I said, don't ask. Get Louise and meet me."

Hanging up, her curiosity unsatisfied, Gloria called out. "Louise, Lester's got a yen to see the Everglades. We're meeting him in Belle Glade. Don't ask questions 'cause I don't have any answers." She drove her 1941 black Ford Business Coupe to Muck City, as Gloria called Belle Glade.

Belle Glade was blessed, or cursed, with dark mineral-rich soil which produced sugarcane, a major lucrative crop in the area. It was a blessing to the landowner who profited, but a curse to the workers who labored in it.

Louise grew up deprived and living in squalor in Belle Glade. After her mother abandoned the family, she cared for her two younger sisters.

After an hour's drive, Gloria spotted Lester standing beside his car with the trunk open. When they parked behind him, he reached in the trunk and lifted out a large can.

"Lester, why are we here? You know I, I ..." Louise stammered, overwhelmed with a rush of memories. Whenever those memories forced their way to her consciousness, she cried over them. Just like now. Tears poured down her face, ruining her makeup.

Lester clasped Louise's hand in his and led her through the overgrown grass and weeds to an abandoned, dilapidated house. A crooked hand printed sign hung by a rusted nail. Local hunters had peppered it with buckshot.

NO TRESSPASSING
This Means You

Lester unscrewed the cap on the can he carried. A pungent, sweet aroma rose in the air, the unmistakable smell of gasoline. He kicked in what remained of the front door and poured the liquid throughout the first floor of the wooden structure. Then he handed Louise a pack of matches.

"I bought this place today for the back taxes. It's time to let go. Go ahead."

Without hesitation, Louise struck the match and dropped it. In minutes, the hungry flames roared, eating everything in their path, setting the house ablaze.

Lester was less emotional, but just as committed as Louise.

Lester, Gloria, and Louise stood united, staring at the fire, listening to the crackle of the greedy flames, the groaning of timber bowing to the inevitable. The few panes of glass popped and shattered. Finally, the roof caved in. It crashed to the ground in a shower of sparks and a cloud of smoke shooting into the sky. As the fire destroyed the house, a funeral pyre of her past, Louise buried the hardships, the disappointments, and the sorrows of the childhood she had endured in silence.

Gloria leaned into Lester and whispered. "This could be *The Hermit Card.* A desire for solitude and self-reflection."

When it was over, Louise loved Lester even more than before.

Lester, Gloria, and Louise were or never would be ham and eggers.

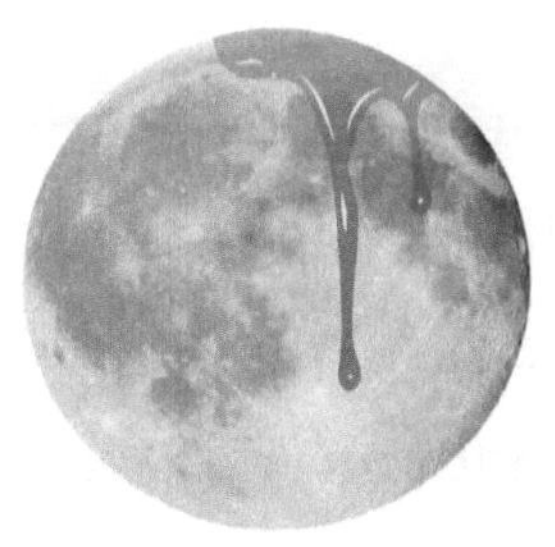

CHAPTER

EIGHTEEN

| DAY 21

The flight to Los Angeles was long and cost a lot of do-re-mi. The government considered air flights a public utility, and the Feds regulated airfares which ensured the airlines always made more than enough profit. Flying from Florida to Los Angeles in a Trans-World Airline Lockheed Constellation was down to thirteen hours, four minutes, and twenty seconds, if you're counting. And Lester and Gloria were counting, making every minute speak for itself.

The limo drivers lined up in the outer concourse in the arrivals section stood at attention in their full uniform of black suit, white shirt, black tie and chauffer's hat, like soldiers for morning arms inspection. Each held signs with the names of their assigned pickup. Neither had this royal treatment before.

Frenchie arranged for an Abracadabra Studio limousine to meet them and take them to the Hollywood Plaza Hotel, a 198-room luxury property on Vine Street. The Hollywood mainstay was the home of many movie stars and a radio show broadcast from the top of the ten-story tower.

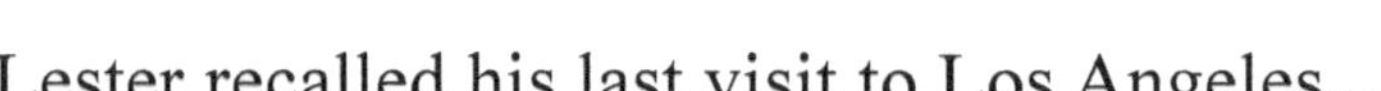

Lester recalled his last visit to Los Angeles...

The 1940s brought tremendous change to the Golden State. California became a shop and aircraft manufacturing hub. Urban population soared. New communities were born overnight as workers and their families arrived to staff the new and expanded factories. As an NYPD Detective, Lester flew out to extradite Milton Halifax, a fugitive wanted for the murder of his wife and her lover.

He shot them each in the head. Their naked bodies were found, as he'd discovered them during their carnal pleasure act. It was easy for Milton Halifax to hide among the vast population of about 1,500,000 people. The city was like a huge nest of ants scurrying here and there. Ants had a purpose. People ... some did, and some didn't.

Milton tried to pose as an ordinary citizen among the everyday populace who had a job and family. It worked for a few years until a first-class citizen saw his wanted poster hanging in the lobby of the United States Post Office–Los Angeles Terminal Annex, 900 North Alameda Street.

The citizen worked with Milton. The reward was too great to pass up. Besides, he knew Milton would never be back in Los Angeles once he was in custody and returned to Miami. Milton thought he had escaped the wrath of the law and the consequences of his actions.

Lester walked into Milton's place of employment, an offshoot of one of the airlines. It was a busy area. Men and women trained as machinists were diligently working. The shop steward led Lester, two L.A. detectives, and three uniform cops through the factory. As they marched through each section, everyone stopped working, turning their heads to follow each step. The worker next to Milton saw the entourage approaching and called his attention to the procession. No one knew their purpose except Milton. Capture was easy. Milton shut his machine down and stood without fanfare or token resistance. Lester cuffed his hands behind his back. Milton turned his head as he passed the person who had turned him in, the only one who kept his head down, his machine running, and continued working.

A bellhop showed Lester and Gloria to their room. No check in. Their pre-arranged accommodation was carte blanche, first class all the way. All their expenses were paid down to dry cleaning, laundry and shoeshine. Gloria undressed for the shower, glancing at the clock. The sun had set. It was 8 p.m. West Coast time and 11p.m. Palm Beach time. She walked to Lester, pressing her naked body against his back while he poured them a nightcap. She reached for him, locating exactly what she wanted.

Lester needed no encouragement. He couldn't deny it felt good ... great. *She always knew when and what to do to get what she wanted,* he thought. Usually, their desires ran in parallel lines. It was okay with him. Exhaustion had no part here.

She whispered his name. "You know, Lester, if your 'what if,' about the Ruby Russell dinner party leaving and circling back doesn't fit, this fits." She continued what she started.

Tension gripped each of them. Pleasure was moments away. Gloria removed each piece of clothing Lester wore, slowly, methodically, button by button, all the while backing him toward the bed. Gloria's enthusiasm was just one quality men loved about her, including Lester.

He stroked her cheek softly with one finger. His kiss, gentle, his tongue traced the seam of her lips. He stroked her back in a way that made her wriggle with delight.

She felt a cool tingle run over her skin, down to her toes she had never felt before with anyone, not even Lester until now.

He rolled her gently on her back. His eyes noticed her tawny complexion for the first time, smooth as silk, inviting his touch. *She is really beautiful.*

Gloria was euphoric. *Is this affirmation, doubt, or ... could I be in love? Is this what Pamela referred to when I stopped her turning cards at number six? Am I Aphrodite or Venus, goddess of love?*

Neither saw the red blinking light, signaling there was a message.

CHAPTER

NINETEEN

Lester rolled over, waking to the California morning sunlight streaming through the windows. *Christ! Bright sun, red blinking light. Probably room service with megawatt smiles too.* Alert and annoyed by the unscheduled wake-up call and the message light, he pressed the button on the telephone to hear the message.

"Mr. Caine. Please call as soon as you are awake. The time difference and travel lag is a bother. I have done it many times. You get used to it. I will send a car to you for the funeral. That's why you're here and I assume for other investigation work."

Second message: "Sorry, I didn't identify myself. This is Frenchie. Here's my number."

"Jesus, Gloria, we need to get moving. It's 7 a.m. here."

"Okay. I just want to savor the moment. Give me a minute to enjoy," she whispered, stroking his chest and admiring his tattoo of Lady Justice holding the scales. *Wisdom* scrolled beneath her feet. "Start the shower. I'll be right behind you after I call room service for coffee."

The Studio limo was waiting to escort them to the Forever Cemetery on Santa Monica Boulevard, just doors away from the Abracadabra Studios, United Artists, Paramount, RKO, NBC, and Columbia. Just south, near Venice Boulevard, was MGM and 20th Century Fox on Pico Boulevard.

This was Hollywood's film making mecca where Ruby Russell had been the Goddess of the Silver Screen. No scripted film would be shot this day—only the news cameras that would broadcast this event on every evening news, splashed all over the tabloids, the rag papers like the *Yellow Press* and television. Coverage of Ruby Russell's funeral was all about the Benjamins, who could get it broadcast and printed first, and what freelance stringers could sell the photos to the highest bidder.

Police motorcycle cops escorted the cortege through the streets lined block after block after block with mourners, stretching for miles. The Abracadabra studio had specially painted the ruby red hearse to carry Ruby to her ultimate resting place past thousands of her adoring fans. Lester's cynical thoughts wondered if the city cleanup crews would remember her as fondly as he watched fans tossing flowers and holding signs of love and admiration as they paid their respects to their beloved actress.

Their limo turned into 6000 Santa Monica Boulevard. Huge fan palm trees, over fifty feet tall, lined the street and welcomed the cars with style and grace, just as the peaceful site and spirits of the deceased buried there greeted anyone who entered with their special grace.

The grounds were beautiful. Peacocks strutted near a lake, flaunting and rattling their train of feathers. [9]

"It seems a pity to have it like this," Lester said, looking out at the sea of graves that lined the lawns.

"What do you mean?"

"There's no other way out. It doesn't matter who you are, what you have or don't have, where you come from, or how wealthy you are. This is it. The end for everyone. Un-noticed souls."

---

[9] When a peacock spreads its feathers in a complex display to attract mate, communicate with other peacocks and intimidate predators.

"Your mother would love it here, Lester. She would talk to everyone who would give her the time. No one unnoticed," Gloria said, meaning the dead spirits.

"You're right, Gloria. Pamela would love it. I should bring her here."

The limousine was just for the two of them. The driver's partition closed. Neither bothered to press the call button requesting he lower the screen.

"Being among the dead is disquieting," Gloria said.

"Maybe it's a glance in the crystal ball of our future, when we become another un-noticed soul."

The procession stopped, and the limo drivers opened car doors simultaneously, like they were choreographed. The attendees were directed to the stunning Cathedral Mausoleum where oversized statues of the Twelve Apostles stood on the marble floor, illumined by sunlight through the ceiling-to-floor-stained glass windows.

"Lester, there are so few people here. You'd think half the world would be packed in here. You know, dignitaries, pols, other film stars. She whispered not to be heard during a quiet moment when the priest officiated over the urn of Ruby's ashes.

"Yeah, you'd think. With all the fuss of a special painted hearse, procession and the fans thronging the streets, I didn't expect this process to be so private. Amélie said Ruby had it in her will to keep her service small."

"I guess from seeing what's here compared to the thousands that lined the street who want to be here, it's small, quaint," Gloria said.

"Maybe fifty or sixty. What the hell. That lying bitch!" Lester barely kept from jumping up and shouting.

"Shush!" Gloria gripped his arm. "What?" whispering.

"Frenchie said her makeup artist would get Ruby ready for her public to keep her beautiful. She had her cremated."

"Well, there goes our chance at more evidence in case we had to exhume her. What's the saying? Can't get blood from a stone. Do you see who I see?" Gloria asked.

"Sure, do. Cozy, isn't it? All the dinner guests are sitting together."

"You're right. Do you think that happened by chance?"

"You know how I feel about chance ... never., Birds of a feather flock together," Lester sneered.

"They're doing more than flocking. Looks more like nesting. I wonder how close they really are."

Lester grinned. "I'd say they're very familiar with each other," thinking of Mrs. Thomson's foot rub on his leg.

CHAPTER

TWENTY

The limos drove everyone to the Abracadabra Studios. Thirty-six sound stages, eleven exterior sets, a photographer's studio, wardrobe, make-up, private dressing room trailers for the stars, ranging from ten feet to forty feet, depending on their status. Ruby Russell and John Arthur had merited forty feet of luxury.

Amélie had arranged a catered lunch in Sound Stage One, the largest and Ruby's favorite stage. A who's who of box office actors, actresses, directors, producers, and studio bigwigs, as well as employees who had worked with and knew Ruby from behind the cameras to stunt people, extras, security, and hangers-on packed the place. Well over 500 people, by Lester's estimate.

"Well, Lester, here's the crowd we thought would be at the cemetery. Now what?"

"Hell, if I know. We need to work the room. Mingle and listen for anything that will get us to Chang. Keep an eye on our flock of birds. I'm hoping they'll slip up as they drink. I'll start left; you go right. We'll meet in the middle—sometime," he directed.

"First things first. I'm going to the bar. Care to join me?"

"Why not? It's five o'clock somewhere."

The crowd was loud and growing louder with each trip to the open bar. Four gigantic screens showed film clips of Ruby. The twenty-six-piece orchestra played. Would anyone spew a eulogy? Would anyone hear them if they were so inclined? This gathering resembled a party disguised as a wake to celebrate Ruby the way only they knew how, Hollywood style. All the praise had been said and done at the cemetery as Ruby wanted.

The orchestra began its first song with the Ruby Waltz. The noise abated, silenced. Everyone there knew the song and knew Ruby. Focused on the screens, seeing

Ruby alive doing what she did best, giving of herself to the public. She brought tears, happiness and messages of hope, forgiveness, and love in her performances and in her movies. The orchestra swung right into its repertoire of musical scores from all of Ruby's movies. People mingled, joked, danced. Drinks spilled; people laughed. It was not just a party; it was a gala honoring, Ruby Russell.

Lester turned to express his "I'm sorry," at the bump jostling the arm holding his Jim Beam. Surprised, he heard, "Well, hi handsome. Fancy meeting you here."

"Well, 'Of all the gin joints in all the towns in all the world, she walks into mine,'" Lester said.

"A man who quotes great lines from great movies from great actors," she replied.

"Why not? I dig Bogart. "

"Let's dance." She signaled to a passing waiter, placed their drinks on his tray, and led Lester to the dance floor. Although he led, she pulled him in real close.

"Do you want to meet him?"

"Who?" Lester asked.

"Bogie. He's here. He's a friend. Or maybe you'd like me to show you around a little. Grab another drink for us and meet me at that door," pointing.

"Show me around first," he said, hoping she would slip up with another drink, maybe reveal something vital to his investigation. She seemed eager to be his best friend, playing footsy under the table during their interview.

"I'll be back with the drinks," he said. "Don't go away."

The door led to the back lot where all the Star trailers lined up like a car dealership showing off the new year models.

"I know how to get into them, and the security guard knows me."

"You seem to know your way around a lot of people, Mrs. Thomson."

"You can call me Lizzy–from Elizabeth. All my friends do. What shall I call you? Les?"

"Lester."

"Alright, Lester. This way."

She used a key to open a trailer door. "This is, or was, Ruby's, Lester. I thought you'd enjoy seeing it. Don't spill your drink. Ruby kept it immaculate. She employed her own staff to keep it that way, her way. Sit down, take a load off. Loosen your tie, relax. This party will go on for, who knows how long?"

Lizzy moved closer to Lester. "Cheers," she said, touching her glass to his. And placing her hand on his knee.

"What are we toasting?" Lester asked.

"We're here together and may become really close ... friends."

"Where is Mr...."

"Shh." Lizzy whispered, placing her finger on Lester's lips. "Mr. Thomson is somewhere out there, and we are in here," she said, loosening his tie. Suddenly, a loud metallic pounding repeated on the trailer door–like a male woodpecker imitating a frenzied drummer.

BANG- BANG -BANG- BANG -BANG -BANG- BANG -BANG

"Lizzy, I know you're in there. This is the last time I'm warning you. I will call the cops."

"All right, all right, Clarence. I'm coming out," she answered. "He's the security guard. He takes his job too seriously," she said to Lester.

"Give me those keys. How the hell did you get these?" Clarence asked. "Goddamn you, Lizzy. I could get fired. Now get out of here. The next time I see you on the back lot, I will have security escort you out and charge you with trespassing. Leave now!"

"I'm going, Clarence. Calm your drawers. Here are the keys."

"You too, fella. Get off this back lot." He continued to mumble garbled warnings.

"I guess we have to dance, Lester. Let's join the party."

Mr. Thomson cut in on Lester's dance with Mrs. Thomson, and Gloria stepped in to take her place.

"Anything?" Gloria asked. "Your tie's loose. Care to explain?"

"No, not really," intentionally neglecting to mention what Lizzy really wanted of him. "How about on your end?"

"The only thing on my end was that midget, who grabbed my ass while we danced. I couldn't even knee him in his balls, he was so little. So, I slapped him. He ran off like a scolded puppy. I don't want anyone touching my ass except you. I scoured the room, spoke with a lot of the behind-the-scenes people. From my days at Summer Stock, they're the ones who know what's going on and aren't tight lipped. Chang's not here and no one I've spoken to has seen him. Now what?" Gloria said.

"I've got to call Walker. Chang's in the wind. I have to give him more credit than he deserves. It's all pointing to him. But why? He doesn't fit for me. He was going to work in her new movie. What's his motive?" Lester said.

"I bet he's here in Hollywood. Remember him and Amélie in the drawing room that day?"

TWENTY-ONE

DAY 24
THE HOME OF RUBY RUSSELL
SANTA MONICA, CALIFORNIA

Ruby Russell's home was in the residential part of Hollywood known for the homes of its elites—movie stars, directors, producers, studio CEOs—Topanga Canyon in the Santa Monica Mountains, Los Angeles, California. The Canyon offered seclusion, the appearance of a wilderness miles from civilization. It epitomized the easy lifestyle of the famous and the wealthy. Ruby had embraced the laid-back life when she was off set and tucked away, remote from the hustle of movie star life. Known for spectacular mountain and ocean views, many celebrities considered Topanga Canyon their hideaway, as Ruby did until twenty-four days ago.

"Lester, I can't imagine living this lifestyle. It looks so glamorous and yet ... After speaking with Ruby's friends and associates, it must have been a tough life. It took dedication, discipline and hard work. This was her reward." Gloria said.

"Yes, Ma'am. Topanga is a beautiful place. It's the name given to the area by the Native American Tongva tribe. Topanga means where the mountain meets the sea," said the limo driver as the Abracadabra Studio limo rolled into the circular drive.

"It's nice that you know the history of the area," Lester said.

"Yes, sir, thank you. My mother's ancestors are from the Tongva tribe. I'm proud of my heritage," he said, stepping out to open the doors for his passengers.

"And rightly so," Gloria stated.

"I'll wait for you in the guest house until you're ready to leave. Just pick up the guest phone. It's ruby red. You can't miss it."

Ruby's home was an Italian-style villa with an oversized Roman pool. A waterfall flowing into both circular ends immediately caught Lester's eye. The surrounding trim tile was ruby red. He imagined she had held lavish parties beside the pool and the connected ornate garden, manicured by humble hands, just like at her Palm Beach estate.

"Welcome to the home of Ruby Russell," Frenchie said, greeting Lester and Gloria. "Come in. Let me show you around. Ruby purchased this lovely villa from ... excuse me. Ruby never wanted me to say who lived here. All I can say is he was a founder of the Las Vegas strip. You know who I'm speaking of," Amélie said, pushing her nose to one side with her index finger.

Lester remembered some lore that interpreted a gesture resulting in a crooked nose as a crooked person or mobster.

"Look here, just outside the door to your right. See the three bullet holes? *They* missed that time. Eventually, his assassins gunned him down at his girlfriend's house in Las Vegas. She, unfortunately, was in the wrong place at the wrong time or the right place at the wrong time, as the saying goes. Imagine, in her own home. I never understood that. How can you be at the wrong place in your own home? She got blasted by a machine-gun, just like him. Ruby said to leave the bullet holes. It added mystery and romance. All Hollywood knows about it. The L.A. Gazette wrote a feature on it, with Ruby and John Arthur pointing to the bullet holes. Ruby's Hollywood friends in the biz came to visit and had their photo taken next to it."

"A life of crime and a Hollywood star pay more than the phone bill," Gloria said.

"I wanted you to see Ruby had everything to live for. I'm so glad you both are on this investigation," Amélie said, her eyes welling up. "I, I ... have no words for this."

"We understand," Lester said.

"Miss Frenchie, I know this is a terrible shock to you. It must be hard for you ... living in Ruby's house. You must expect her to appear at any time. You realize this is now a homicide investigation?" Gloria said.

"I know, I know. Thankfully, you told me in time for me to issue a statement to the AP through Ruby's PR people. It's too surreal. Considering your background, you may be used to this. I'm on heavy medication to sleep. But who? Why? How could anyone do that and no one hear anything? How could that be?" Amélie asked.

"I'm sorry, Frenchie. We can't answer that yet. Where's Chang?" Lester asked.

"I don't know, Mr. Caine. He said he had to straighten out some SAG union business, so I got the studio plane to fly him out here from Palm Beach. He never showed up at the SAG or the studio office. I'm worried sick about Lei. He didn't come to Ruby's funeral. No one can locate him. I don't understand why you keep asking for him. Do you know where he is, either of you?" Amélie said.

"Well, duh, if we knew, we wouldn't ask you," Gloria said.

Lester threw her a take it down a notch look.

"Frenchie, maybe you'd better sit," Gloria said.

"Oh no. I don't know if I can take another sitting session. The last time I fainted and fell off the couch. Just tell me." She said.

"Alright. The Palm Beach District Attorney issued a warrant for Lei Chang's arrest. He's wanted for the murder of Ruby Russell," Lester answered, moving toward Amélie in case she fainted.

"OH ... MY ... GOD!" she cried out, dropping on the sofa. "It's alright Mr. Caine," holding her hand up to reassure him. "I'm alright. I'm sitting now. Please sit, both of you. Tell me, please."

"All the evidence points to Mr. Chang and now that he's nowhere to be found, it substantiates our findings. The news is going to hit the front pages within a few days, so you better get on top of it with your people. Chang must have figured out that we know. The police photos of the scratches and neck wound show a struggle. The hardware store clerk verified he purchased the rope used to hang Miss Russell after he murdered her. It's him. Besides, he's in the wind. He's slicker than he appeared." Lester said.

"But why? She treated him so well. He had opportunities given to him many would kill for ... Oh, I can't believe I just said *that*," Frenchie sobbed.

"Miss Frenchie, we need to ask you about Chang. Was there anything between Miss Russell and Chang? Were they lovers? Was he in financial trouble? Maybe he wanted to borrow money, and she said no? What can you tell us? Do you have *any* idea where he may be?" Gloria asked.

"None, Miss Saville. I am without words. I handled Ruby's finances, liaised with the studio and her agent. I did it all for Ruby. There was nothing. I would have known. There was nothing. He lives here and at the Palm Beach estate. I've left word to have him or the house staff call the minute he shows up."

"Oh, my god. I'm, I'm so stupid," Amélie stammered. "He has a sister who lives in San Francisco's Chinatown. I could not reach her either. This is not good. Why would he disappear, unless ... Oh, my god. He murdered Ruby! But why? I'm sick. So, he lied to me about needing to straighten out business with SAG and the studio. It was a ruse to use the studio plane and what, disappear? Oh, my God! How could he? I'll give you Chang's sister's address. Don't worry, Mr. Caine. The studio will take care of everything for you," she said.

"Palm Beach Police issued bulletins to all the police stations, train depots, and airports throughout the country and to Interpol. He is still in the country as far as we can tell. So, it's important if you hear from him or get an inkling of where he might be that you contact us immediately. Don't alert him. Do you understand? It's urgent he doesn't suspect you've contacted us," Lester said.

"Of course, Mr. Caine. You know I will help anyway I can."

"We'll need a picture of Chang. A recent one," Gloria said.

"I have one of the three of us–Ruby, Chang and myself. I'll get it for you and his sister's information. Of course."

A CHICKEN'S MODUS OPERANDI... THEY ALWAYS COME HOME TO ROOST!

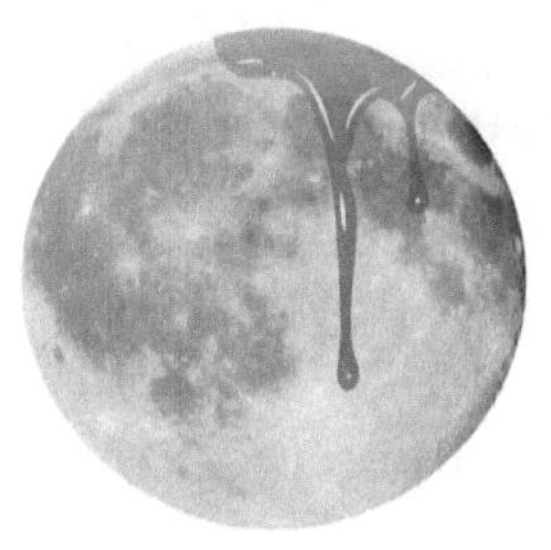

TWENTY-TWO

Lester thought that taking the studio limo would do nothing but bring attention to them and mute the lips of those they needed to speak. The cab dropped them on the corner of Grant Avenue and Stockton Street in the heart of San Francisco's Chinatown. They suspected this was going to be a hellacious undertaking.

Chinatown was a city within a city within a city with fragmented districts, landmarks, and edges of a gritty side. Outsiders were not welcome, and yet there they were. The alleys were narrow and populated with doorways to the brothels and gambling hells. They heard Mah Jong tiles clicking and coins dropping to place bets. None of this was unfamiliar to them.

Lester's thoughts raced to his father's death—killed in a back-alley dice game, shooting *craps* in a West Side Manhattan neighborhood in New York, far from their home in the Bronx. When he was an NYPD Detective, he covered Five Points, a notorious Irish slum. If you believed in a God or deity, they were nonexistent there. It was the Devil's workshop. Davey Crocket himself had named it, 'Hell's Kitchen.' The world and Lester came to know the area by Crockett's label.

And yet they saw another side to Chinatown, right in its center. Tourists poured in with money, shopping for deals, or dined on Asian cuisine. Floor shows in glamorous nightclubs attracted women in sequined gowns with tuxedoed partners while naked dancers strolled through the room. The commercial side of the forbidden city was accepted, even encouraged.

"Jesus, Lester. Look at what's pulling up to these clubs. We could have fit right in with the studio limo," Gloria said, disillusioned.

"Maybe, just maybe, we can grease some palms in this environment and cut to the chase to lead us to Chang," Lester said.

"Good evening. Welcome to the Shanghai Low," said the Maître D'. "Would you like a table?"

"Maybe you can tell me if you've seen this man?" Lester said, showing him the photo Amélie gave them.

"Are you police?"

"No, his sister is worried. She hasn't been able to find him and hired us. He has a very large inheritance, but he must appear in person to collect it." Lester said with a double saw buck under his thumb. It was common practice and a legal one for cops to lie to their suspects. It came naturally.

"Let me see." He took the picture and slipped the twenty-dollar bill from Lester in the same move.

"I know him and her," pointing to Chang and Amélie. "But her, yes. Who would not know Ruby Russell? She's never been here, but the other two come together. I can tell you where the Hollywood stars and the movie businesspeople hang out," he said with a pointed look.

Lester knew all too well what that look meant. He peeled off a ten from his money clip. The Maître D' continued to stare. Lester peeled a second ten spot.

"Thank you," bowing his head. "Usually, the movie crowd is at the Forbidden City Club. That's at the end of the street. They have fabulous shows. You can't miss it. Is there anything else?" he said, dipping his head.

"No, thank you," Lester said.

The Maître D' bowed again and turned away.

The Forbidden City Nightclub and Cabaret, appropriately named, was the night spot of choice for the Hollywood set. Men in tuxedos, and women in mink stoles who glittered with diamonds, spilled out of expensive sports cars and limos, in the heart of Chinatown. The shows included burlesque performers, dancers and singers and attracted Hollywood's who's who, shattering the stigma of a seedy reputation Chinatown once had.

"Gloria, remember why we're here? We've got to keep a clear head in this un-chartered territory," Lester said, scoping out the room. Lola's Jazz Club held some 300 patrons on a packed night. This Club held twice that.

"Lester, this is as bad as the bash in sound stage one at Ruby's memorial party."

"There's too many people to ask everyone at these tables."

Greeted by the Maître D,' and before being escorted to their table, Lester brought out the photo, once again showing just enough of a double sawbuck for the Maître D to understand he was hunting for information.

"Who, what, and where have you seen these people?"

"Oh, yes. Many, many times, I see Miss Russell and always these two with movie star. Many times, with many others, but these two (pointing to Amélie and Chang) always with her and sometimes come by themselves. He famous in China, not so much here. Not a nice man. He thinks he boss, but no, this Miss Amélie boss. He stupid man. Should go back to China. I will miss her. I see paper, so sad. She so nice, big tip." He gave Lester the same pointed look and fake smile as the other Maître D.'

"Have you seen these two lately?" Lester asked, handing him another twenty.

"Only him. He want favor because he bring Miss Russell here. He no bring her. She come here many times before him. He stupid man."

"When? When was he here and what favor did he want?"

"My cousin work on ship. He want cousin to get him on ship. He in movies. Why he want job on ship? He stupid man. I tell him you go now. You have no more boss. Everybody see newspaper. I no want him here. He stupid man. He go."

"What ship does your cousin work on?"

Another direct look, another painted smile, and another twenty.

"Cousin, Mei Ling. I tell him stupid man, no help."

"What's the ship?"

"LÓNGFEI. You ask for Dragonfly. You go waterfront piers south under Bay Bridge, First and Brannan Street. Ship Dock Howard Two."

"Thank you."

He put his hands together as in prayer and bowed.

"Good thing we're on Amélie's dime and can pass it on to her," Lester said.

"Good timing, Lester. We are just in time for a table and the show."

"Next time around, Gloria. For now, we've got to hit the docks."

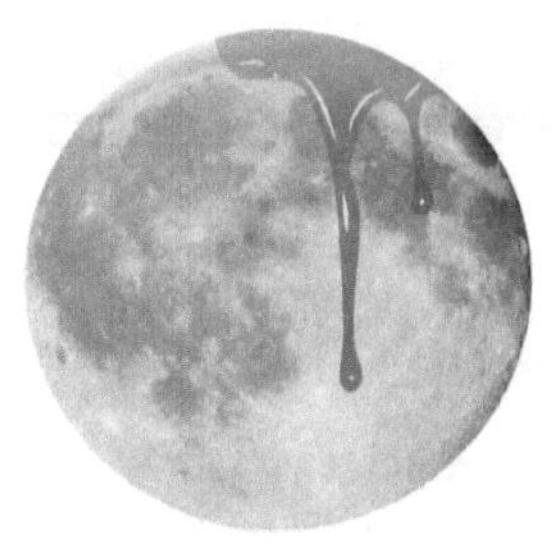

TWENTY-THREE

DOCKS AT SAN FRANCISCO
PIER HOWARD TWO

The cab swung onto the dock. Lester couldn't open the door fast enough to get out, paying the fare with a tip. They did not know when and if the ship would depart.

"Lester, slow down. My shoes are killing me."

"Better your feet are killing you than Chang killing you. C'mon, give me your hand."

They rolled up the gangway, holding on to the side ropes only to be greeted by the Watch Stander, a heavily armed man who lowered his weapon as he saw Lester and Gloria getting closer with each step up the gangway.

"Halt!" they heard in his Chinese Putonghua accent.

"Get your ID ready," Lester commanded.

"We are local police," both flashed their Private Investigator licenses and badges as quickly as possible so the guard would not question them any further.

"What you want here. You no belong here. This Chinese ship. You go."

"We have authority from the United States. We are looking for this man," Lester stated, showing him Chang's photo before the man could question their credentials. "Have you seen him?"

"Me no see. You go."

"You didn't even look. Where is your captain? I'm not leaving until I speak to him," Lester said, showing his credentials again. He knew the guard did not know what he was being shown. Just that he had a badge alongside the P.I.'s license.

"You stay. I call."

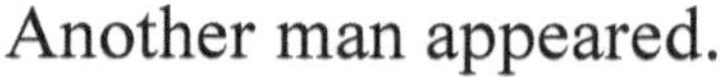

Another man appeared.

"What you want with a Chinese ship?" The man asked.

"I'm looking for this man?" Lester showed Chang's photo.

"This must be man cousin tell me. He stupid man. I no see him. Anything else?"

"Can we look around the ship?" Gloria asked, using her womanly wiles.

"You see," using a sweeping motion with his hand. "This big ship. Can take long, long time. You go with guard." He pointed to Lester. "You," pointing to Gloria, "you come with me. I show you. Better."

"We'll come back with more men to search the ship," Lester said, nodding to Gloria to get moving as he saw armed Chinese men coming on deck.

"You come back, bring paper to search. You hurry. We leave soon," the captain said, mumbling something in Chinese.

"Jesus Christ Lester. I don't scare very easy, but..."

"I hear you, Gloria. That would have been one situation we might not have escaped. I knew what he was aiming at."

"Yeah, me alone with him and I don't know how many after him. Piece of shit."

"Let's ask around the dock. There's usually a Dock Master and there has to be security."

"Let's do this Lester. We have to go back to where the cab dropped us. Remember, he didn't want to approach the guardhouse."

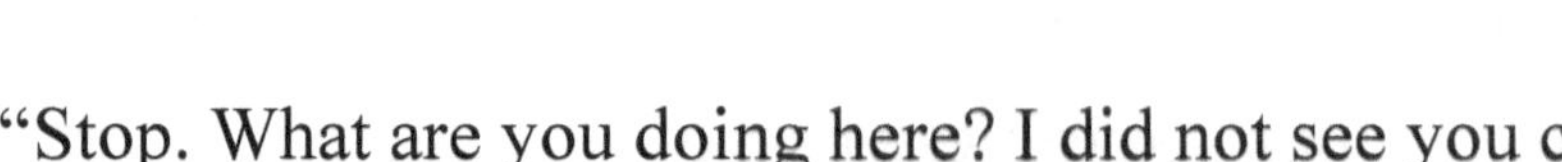

"Stop. What are you doing here? I did not see you come in," the guard said sternly, holding his hand up.

"We're looking for this man," Lester said, showing him Chang's photo.

"VaVaVa Voom, honey! Frisco detectives sure get better looking."

Gloria took one step forward, pulling her jacket aside to show her gun and handcuffs. "It's Detective. We can make this easy or hard. You pick."

"Settle down, Detective. I meant no harm. Yeah, I spotted him earlier today. Had to throw him out. He snuck in on the docks, looking for work. He ain't no union guy. Musta thought the union and the Waterfront Employers Association were still on strike and were looking to hire a scab, you know? That walkout lasted almost one hundred days. A lot of folks were arrested. I had to have him escorted off the property. He was a feisty little bastard. My men waited and made sure he got a cab and drove off. Ain't seen him since. Anything else, *De-tec-tive*," he said with emphasis, staring at Gloria.

"Did you or your men see the taxi?" Gloria questioned.

"What? It's a taxi. They're all the same—DeSoto suburban, yellow and red. You should know. ... Wait ... a ... minute."

"Okay, we're good," Lester said, stepping in to block the guard from leaving his booth, and pulling back his suit jacket to show his gat.

"Let's go, Lieutenant. Leave him be. We're good. We got what we need," Gloria said to diffuse the situation before it could go south.

"You're right, Detective. We're done here." Lester added, "Thanks for your help."

TWENTY-FOUR

| YELLOW CAB COMPANY

Hailing a taxi close to the docks where all the ships came to port, both ocean liners and freighters, was a cinch.

"Where's your dispatch office?" Lester belted out, getting into the taxi.

"Golden Gate and Jones Street," replied the hack.

"Get us there as fast as you can."

"Yes, sir. I'm just about done with my shift so I can kill two birds with one stone," he said. "What's your hurry?"

"We're looking for this man," Gloria said, leaning over the seat and showing the driver Chang's photo.

"No, can't say I've seen him. I take a lot of folks, you know, but not him. Chinese don't take taxis. They ride the trolley and buses that are in full service. Why are you in such a hurry to find him? If you were cops, you wouldn't be ridin' in no cabbie. You must be like a skip tracer, vigilante, or a marshal of some sort, right?"

"You're right. We're private detectives and there's a warrant out for his arrest," Lester said, hoping to get the word out on the street.

"Is there a reward?"

"We could arrange that," Lester said.

"How much?"

"Depends on how soon we catch him," Gloria said, staving him off.

"Here we are. That'll be one dollar and twenty cents, Mister."

"How can I help you?" the dispatcher asked.

"We're looking for this man," Lester said, showing Chang's photo along with his P.I. badge.

"He was just here. You just missed him. He may be in the garage asking the mechanics about work."

They drew their guns, rushing out of the office and into the garage where the taxis were lined up for repairs and the drivers waited between shift changes.

"There he is. Chang! Stop! Police," Lester called out.

Chang turned, and seeing Lester, drew his gun and fired three rounds in succession. Bullets whizzed all around, ripping faster than the sound barrier at 2,700 feet per second.

BLAM BLAM BLAM

The explosion of sound muted their hearing, bouncing through their heads as if caught mid-stanza during the fury of a drummer's solo without a melody. Lester's eyes barely registered the flash of Chang's gun before he returned fire. The sharp, high-pitched crack of car windshields and the ping of metal created chaos. The deafening ringing in their ears added to the cacophony. Seeing the flash from Chang's gun, Lester and Gloria returned fire. The cabbies and mechanics dove for cover. Then there was silence. The odor of the sulfurous burned gunpowder irritated their eyes and compounded their discomfort.

"Gloria, are you alright?" Lester hollered.

"I'm good. You?"

"Yeah, me too."

"There he is," shouted a mechanic. "He's on the ladder to the roof."

Lester jumped on the hood of a cab and grabbed Chang's feet. Chang kicked. Lester swung toward the ladder, holding on to Chang's foot with one hand, trying to grab the ladder with the other. Gloria pointed her gun at Chang, but Lester got in the way of a clear shot. Chang kicked Lester again, and his shoe slipped into Lester's hand. Chang turned his gun at him. Gloria rang off one shot, missing. It ricocheted off the steel ladder and Chang rocketed up the rungs as he'd done as a stuntman in movies. Nose bleeding, Lester climbed the ladder while Gloria ran to the street, tracking Chang along the roof lines. Chang paused and surveyed his escape route. Panicking as Lester climbed onto the roof, he fired an aimless shot. Then he took several steps back and ran to the edge of the roof, jumping to the next building. Lester ran to the roof's edge, looked down, and knew he couldn't make the leap.

Chang was gone in a flash, nearly as quick as the flash that his gun had fired.

Lester confirmed the drivers and mechanics were uninjured and accounted for as they heard police sirens.

"Jesus Christ, Lester. Here's Pamela's *Tower Card* right here, right now. Distraction, turmoil, dangerous situations," Gloria blurted. "I can't wait for the rest of them."

CHAPTER

TWENTY-FIVE

DAY 27
THE HOME OF RUBY RUSSELL
SANTA MONICA

The events of the last month—Ruby Russell's homicide, planning her memorial, the police investigation—the entire incident was too much for Frenchie to grin and bear it. The newspaper reporters were constantly at the door with film crews. Stringers[10] sneaked onto the property, taking photos for magazines and yellow journalism papers, and selling them to the highest bidder. Amélie had to hire extra security, so she greeted Lester and Gloria with hostility.

[10] Freelance photographers called Stringers only paid for each photo accepted by the newspaper.

"Oh, my god, now it's you two," she snarled.

"Who'd you expect, President Truman?" Gloria snapped back with sarcasm.

"Who knows the way the hordes of people are coming and going here? He could show up."

"Remember, you and the studio hired us. We're here for you," Lester said.

"I know, and I could fire you. I'm sorry. I don't know why I said that. I didn't mean it. I, It ... It's overwhelming," she stammered. "So, you're here. Why ... why are you here? I don't know if I'm coming or going anymore."

"Chang is on the run. He obviously knows he's wanted for murdering Miss Russell. We haven't figured out his motive, why he did it. Can you?" Lester asked.

"No. I told you that. You asked me already. Did you find Lei?"

"He's in San Francisco, reportedly attempting to get on a freighter. He's trying to leave the country," Gloria said.

"Yesh, we found him alright," Lester said. "We spent the past twenty-four hours at the San Francisco Police station. We almost had him, but he shot his way out. Damn lucky no one was hurt. Just a lot of property damage."

"I feel faint," Frenchie said, sitting quickly. "That was Lei? Reports of a gunman shooting up the taxicab company are all over the news. Oh, my god. He shot at you?"

"That was Lei alright. Did you know he is so dangerous?" Gloria said.

Frenchie didn't answer. She looked dazed.

"We think he'll try to contact you. He needs money and a way out of the country. Has he reached out to you?" Lester said.

"I have gotten no messages. He could try the studio, this home which also connects to the Palm Beach house, and my answering service, but I got nothing from any of them. This is so unreal, like I'm in a dream."

"Well, it can't be too long before he gets more desperate. He tried to grab a job on a Chinese freighter to pay for his passage to China. But no one will take him. So, where can he get his hands on cash?" Lester said.

"Oh my God," Frenchie wailed. "This is a movie in the making. I still can't fathom that Lei would do such a thing ... and never to Ruby. Why?"

"That's what we intend to find out, Miss Frenchie," Gloria assured her. "Can you think of anyone, I mean anyone, no matter how outside his orbit, he would try to contact if not you?" Gloria asked again.

"Just his sister. I gave you her name and address. Did you go there?"

"Actually, Frenchie, the FBI is now involved because he crossed state lines. He's a wanted fugitive. They will knock on her door. If she doesn't answer, they will break it down. Have you contacted her in any way? She should not know about the FBI until they get there," Lester said.

"Oh, my God. Now the FBI. There is no way to contact her except by going to her apartment. She has no phone. She is poor, like most Chinatown residents. Lei used to send her money. I need a drink. Can I get you one? I've got to call the studio," she said.

"Sure. A stiff drink might do us all some good. I need to use the phone too. I should call Lieutenant Walker," Lester said.

"We have to stay close. We'll be at the hotel. You or any studio people get in touch with us immediately if you hear from Chang. Do you understand?" Gloria said.

"Yes, yes, of course. I meant to tell you, the Abracadabra Studio is holding a press conference tomorrow. I'll have the studio limo pick you up."

"We'll be ready. Oh, by the way, Miss Frenchie, do you drive a Lincoln Continental convertible?" Gloria asked.

"I don't own any cars, Miss Saville."

"But you have access to the cars the studio owns, I take it. I love those convertibles. Lester drives one. Can you use those cars they have that they use in the movies?"

"I could, but usually I use the studio limousine."

"We'll be ready for tomorrow's press conference," Lester said.

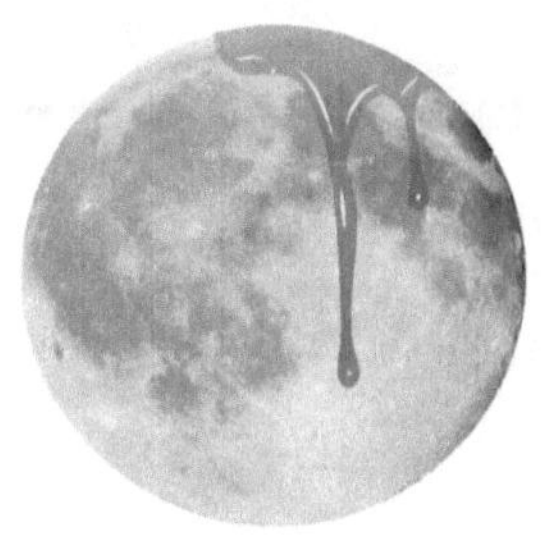

TWENTY-SIX

The FBI certainly proved the famous aphorism of one time President Theodore Roosevelt, when he said, "Speak softly and carry a big stick; you will go far." The Federal Bureau of Investigation did just that and added to its reputation of capturing notorious and nefarious criminals such as Al Capone, Bonnie and Clyde, "Machine Gun" Kelly, John Dillinger, Pretty Boy Floyd, and Ma Barker, just to name a few. Most times, when and if the FBI came knocking, their reputation held that big stick. They began by softly speaking to reason.

Some listened; some did not. As for the aforementioned, many refused to listen to reason, resisted the big stick, and died. They learned the fatal lesson they could not prevail, thus enhancing the FBI's reputation.

"Who is it?"

"FBI. Open the door."

"What you want? I do nothing wrong. I have papers."

"Liánbāng diàochá jú tègōng dǎ kāimén, fǒuzé wǒmen jiāng pòmén ér rù[11]

"Yes, yes. Me open."

The two agents pushed their way in. One sat Yu Yīng down while the other quickly looked around. She lived in a tiny rundown, unheated, one-room flat with a shared bathroom at the end of the hall. Paint hung in little curls, peeling off the ceiling from a previous water leak. She had set mouse traps to catch the mice that came from the

---

[11] "FBI agents open the door or we will break open." (The FBI compiled techniques for conducting interviews by using agents according to ethnicity and religion obtaining confessions and information.)

restaurant three floors below on the street. It took little time to clear the place. Chang wasn't there.

"You speak English. Where is your brother?"

"Me no know. He no here. You see. He come for money. In big hurry. I give him. No say what he need. I know he big Chinese Pai Gow gambler. I think owe big man money."

"Who is big man?"

She shrugged. "Many big man head of Pai Gow.[12]

"We'll be back."

In here lies Pamela's *Page of Pentacles Card.* Wasteful, illogical, rebellious young man, has loss of money.

---

[12] Pai gow-Chinses gambling game played with 32 Chinese dominoes. Originating during Song dynasty.

CHAPTER

TWENTY-SEVEN

The announcement of the Abracadabra Studio's press conference drew every TV station in the Los Angeles viewing area along with a dozen newspapers. Helen Tilly from Palm Beach got wind of it through her Associated Press affiliates and caught a flight to Hollywood.

"Thank you for coming. I'm sorry this is not an announcement for a new Ruby Russell film release. We all know why you're here. My name is Roger Puglia. I am President of Abracadabra Studios. Standing next to me is Jonathan Deinhart, president of Planet Productions. This is not easy for anyone. Ruby Russell was America's sweetheart. She brought joy, laughter, real tears, and love to each of us. Not only will we miss her for her grand performances on the silver screen, but as Ruby the person. She was one of a kind, warm, loving, caring and giving of herself. Her generosity is well known, particularly to children's hospitals. Abracadabra Studios, along with Planet Productions, is offering a $50,000 reward for the capture, arrest, and conviction of this man." Turning, he pointed to the jumbo screen and the image of Lei Chang.

The crowd gave a collective gasp. Flash bulbs lit the air like Fourth of July fireworks.

"His name is Lei Chang. We are now open for questions."

Pandemonium ensued. The reporters yelled, clamoring for attention. All wanted to be recognized first and their question answered.

"Who is this man?"

"How do you know he's the one?"

"Did he know Miss Russell?"

"What was his relationship to Miss Russell?"

"Will they return him to Palm Beach, where the murder took place?"

"Was he Ruby's lover?"

"Wasn't he her bodyguard?"

"Are the L.A. police taking part in the manhunt?"

" Was it true Miss Russell was nude when they found her?"

"Were there any witnesses?"

"What is the evidence?"

"Didn't she commit suicide?"

"Is Chang armed and dangerous? Is he the guy that shot up the Yellow Cab Company?"

"Where are the police looking? Is he here in Los Angeles?"

Puglia waved his hands palms down, giving the crowd the settle down signal.

"Settle down, settle down, please settle down. We will not leave until we've answered every question. You," he pointed. "We will start with you."

"I'm Helen Tilly, reporter for the Miami Journal. Why is Lester Caine, a Private Investigator from Florida, there with you? Is he working with the L.A. Police? Are the Palm Beach Police and the L.A. Police cooperating on this investigation?"

Her questions were taking on an edge.

He replied, "Yes, he is. Next..."

Photographers turned to Lester, snapping his picture and aiming their questions at Lester and to Puglia repeatedly.

"I will have order," Puglia demanded. "If you don't settle down, I will end this press conference."

Helen Tilly wormed her way through the crowd, inching herself close to Lester.

"Well, Lester. Fancy meeting you here. What do you have for me? C'mon Lester, for old times' sake. Give me something."

"Lester's done with old times' sakes, Helen," Gloria said, stepping in.

"Well, Gloria. You're here too. What a shame. I thought..."

"I know what you thought, so fuck off," Gloria snarled.

"Okay, honey. Don't get your britches in a knot. Although I'm sure Lester knows how to untie them," Helen snapped in return.

Lester stepped in between Gloria and Helen to prevent Gloria from flattening Tilly where she stood. They didn't need more publicity.

"Ease up, ladies, and I'm using the term loosely." Lester stepped in, eager to ward off the tension. "We all want the same thing, don't we? Get Chang?" As a New York cop, he'd had to snuff out lots of wicks that were ignited before he and his partner reached the scene. Many of those potential crises were domestic violence calls. Some with guns, some with stickers, and some with explosives. New York City was a tough town.

"You know what I can do to help, Lester. I'm staying at the Hollywood Roosevelt Hotel. You know where you can find me. Nice seeing you. Gloria," she said, sauntering off, but turning and tossing out her departing words. "Hey, my bed has room for three."

Gloria curled her lip and, raising her hand, gave her a one-finger salute. Her middle finger standing at attention.

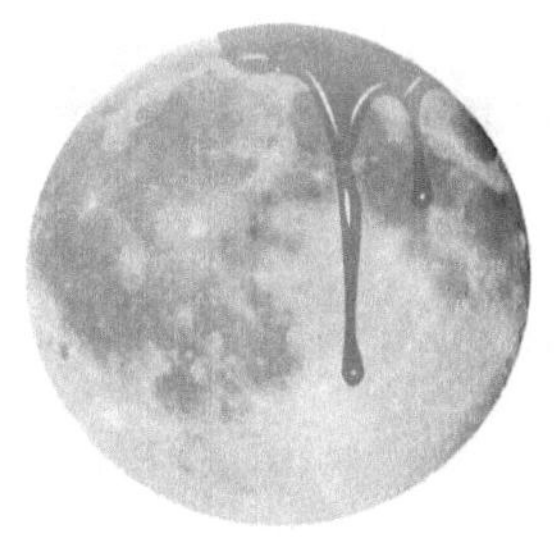

TWENTY-EIGHT

| DAY 30

The TV stations flashed Lei Chang's photograph and segments of the press conference—specifically, Roger Paglia, the head of Abracadabra Studios and Johnathan Deinhart, President of Planet Productions, announcing the reward of $50,000.

Dozens of tips poured in to the police hotline set up for that purpose. The L.A. police monitored the hotline and daily reported any viable leads to the FBI. When more than one enforcement agency is involved, there are always turf wars and struggles about who's running the show. The entity carrying the big stick and speaking softly came out on top more often than not.

A tally of the reports called in pointed to Chang hanging around Chinatown. Reportedly, he was looking for a way out of the country. Seen in first one location, then another, he appeared not to have a permanent hole to hide in. Most of the calls pointed at Yu Yīng, Chang's sister. The FBI set up surveillance on her place and followed her to the Chinese laundry where she worked, and back home; food shopping, back home; to the laundry and back home, establishing a pattern. They came up with nothing.

From his days as a bachelor in New York City, Lester used the Chinese Laundry in New York City's own Chinatown. He would not do his own laundry, would not wash and iron, particularly his dress shirts. So, he brought them to the laundry where they washed, starched, pressed and folded his dress shirts. Then they wrapped them in a neat brown paper bundle and tied it with twine, completing the process. If you didn't have the drop-off ticket or lost it, "no tickie,-no shirtie," was the rule. Lester had observed customers arguing with the owner of the shop, who prevailed because he had the power of the big stick, the shirts in his possession.

Lester and Gloria set up their own surveillance on Yu Yīng, apart from the San Francisco Police Department and the FBI. He knew people were creatures of habits, many of which couldn't be dismissed. It's the nature of the human psyche. He had Gloria drop off a few of his shirts to be laundered. Gloria's summer stock experience earned her the nom de plume of Scarecrow. She was a master of disguise, prominent and yet unrecognizable, like a scarecrow in the field. Neither the FBI nor the SFPD could make her. Yu Ying conducted herself in a shy, polite, and humble manner while dealing with the customers.

Gloria entered the shop to pick up Lester's shirts and did as Lester directed. "See if there are any packaged shirts on the shelf that are missing a ticket number for pickup." Gloria did just that, scanning the shelf as Yu Yīng looked for Lester's ticket number.

"Isn't that it?" Gloria said, pointing to the brown paper package without a ticket number on it.

"No. No you. This you," she said, bringing the package to the counter.

"I don't think so. May I see what's in that package? I think that's my husband's," Gloria insisted.

"No. This, you here. See ticket same," Yu Yīng said.

"Oh, now I see. I'm sorry. Thank you," Gloria said, taking the package of shirts.

"You were right, Lester. There was one package without a ticket on it. I said I thought it was my husband's. She emphatically told me, 'no.' That package didn't have a ticket, and she showed me your package matched the ticket I gave her."

"So, those must be Chang's clothes. He's hiding in her apartment, probably threatened her. Let's wait to see if she takes the bundle to her place."

They waited until Yu Yīng and three others closed the shop. Yu Yīng had the brown paper package with twine tucked under her arm and headed to the corner market where bushels of fruits and vegetables sat open on wooden makeshift benches exposed like the back of a hospital gown. She loitered, picking up and putting down fruit, only selecting the ones she thought were kissed by god.

Lester and Gloria followed Yu Yīng. Daily shoppers buy for themselves every day, but Yu Yīng headed to her third-floor apartment with two brown bags—shirts and two pieces of fruit. One for her and one for her brother. Lei Chang had to be staying with her.

"Lester, what do you think? Take her as she opens the door,"

"Let's give her a half a flight on us."

Yu Yīng approached her stairwell to the hallway leading to her door. Lester and Gloria did double time to reach her as she turned the key to open the rickety door l into her apartment.

Gloria pushed her aside while Lester burst in, gun drawn, hurriedly going through the two rooms.

"Lei no here, Lei no here. He go," Yu Yīng said through tears trembling at Gloria's gun in her face.

"Be quiet and stay there. Don't move," Gloria ordered, standing over her, looking back and forth at Yu Yīng and into the apartment, pushing the door to expand her vision.

"Lester, you good?"

"Yeah. He's not here. He must have been watching from the window. It's open. I'm going up the fire escape. Cover me. She won't do anything."

Gloria turned to enter the apartment. Yu Yīng ran, leaving the brown paper bags on the floor. A man's shirt, presumably Lei's, spilled out of one and the two pieces of fruit rolled into the hallway from the other.

"I'm right behind you, Lester. She took off."

They climbed the rusted metal fire escape that had not seen maintenance or inspection in the last decade. Bolts screeched and eased away from the building wall. Guns drawn; they climbed rapidly up the ladder to the roof. Lester peered above the roof line and ducked back to safety.

Bam-Bam-Bam

Shots rang out. Fragments of the bricks that lined the edge of the roof bounced and fell over the side. Lester held his gun over the edge toward the gunman and returned fire blindly.

Bam-Bam-Bam
SILENCE...

"Lester, are you hit?"

"No, Gloria," Lester said, popping up and rolling onto the tarpaper roof.

"God damn it. He's gone. He must have jumped to the other connecting roof. Look down, see if you see him on the street."

"I guess being a stuntman has its perks," Gloria muttered. "Lester, Pamela's *Moon Card* is in play, telling you that you're unaware of the path you're taking and there could be danger lurking in its depths. We need to cover each other."

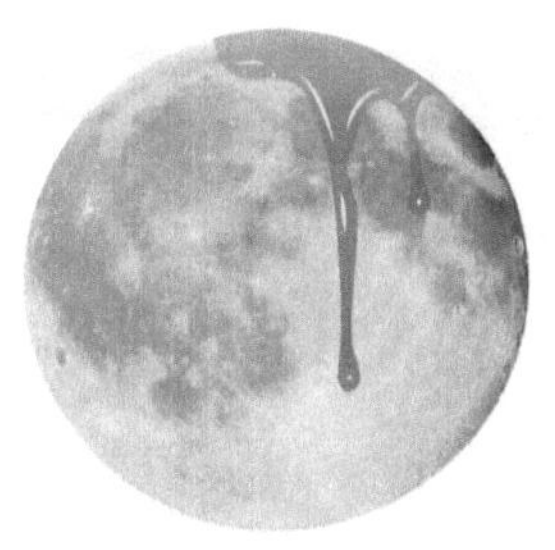

CHAPTER

TWENTY-NINE

The knocking sounded like cracks of thunder.

BANG-BANG–BANG-BANG-BANG.

"Jesus Christ, Lester, who the hell could be banging on our door?"

"Hell, if I know, Gloria. Why don't you find out? Better take your friendly persuader along. You never know who's hiding behind the door," he smirked.

Gloria threw on her robe to cover her nakedness.

"Who is it?" she asked, peering through the spyhole.

"Gloria? It's me, Helen. Helen Tilly. Open the door. Please let me in." Gloria opened the door slowly, her .38 snub nose revolver in her hand.

Helen shoved her way in. "The cops and FBI are all over Chang's sister's apartment. They have her in custody and they're tearing her place apart. What have you two done?"

"What are you talking about?" Lester asked, getting up out of bed, not covering himself from the night's sexual games.

"Jesus, Lester. I was hoping for a more discreet knowledge of your anatomy, maybe followed by carnal knowledge. One where I took part," Helen retorted. "Take your time getting a robe on. I don't mind."

Gloria's eyes narrowed and her eyebrows furrowed at what she regarded as her man being ogled by another female.

Lester knew that look too well.

"GLORIA," Lester warned. Gloria would not hesitate to lay Helen out on the floor and step over her if she fell in her way.

"I'll bet your prints are all over the place. They'll put an APB out for you, wanting to know why you did what you did without informing them. I tried to get some photos of Yu Yīng and her place. My photographer kept shooting film when we saw you ducking bullets. Knowing you were fired upon could save your hide. I know why you were shooting, but the Fibbees will want to know. I have the proof. So, you know, it will be me that saves you from a situation that could turn sour. I'll include you, too, Gloria. Don't worry."

"GLORIA," Lester shouted, seeing her grind her teeth, seething with anger.

"You better get dressed. I expect them to come knocking on your door," Helen said.

"I guess a thank you is in order, Helen. Thank you. See your way out, please. Gloria, get ready. We need to go to the FBI. I'm going in the shower," he said, dropping his robe.

Helen stood admiring the view, her eyes devouring Lester until Gloria called from the open door. "Helen, time to leave."

"Okay, okay, I'm going. Don't get your panties in a knot. Oh, I almost forgot. You're not wearing any."

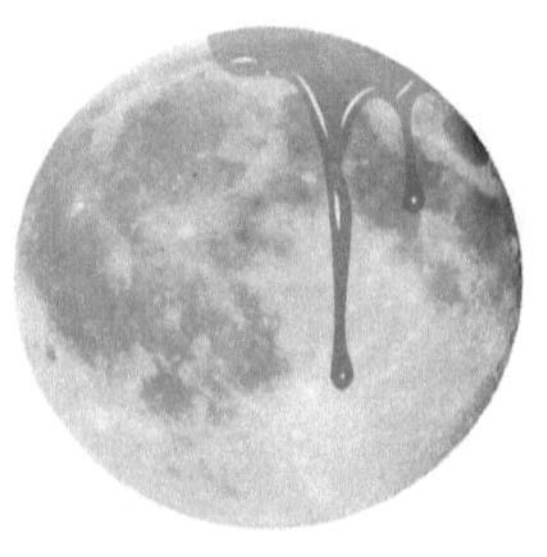

THIRTY

FBI FIELD OFFICE
SAN FRANCISCO

The Hollywood Plaza Hotel doorman blew his whistle, flagging a taxi for Lester and Gloria.

"Fifty United Nations Plaza," Lester called out, crouching as he followed Gloria into the back seat of the cab.

"Going to the Federal Building, are you? So you know, we just got a fare increase," he said, pushing the lever down to start the meter running and clock the distance. "Are you agents? I've had several in my cab who were from out of town and stayed at the hotel. Never a lady before, you know? You must be pretty special," said the cabby.

Lester's thoughts raced. *You have no idea, pal. She's special alright.*

"It's not easy. You know ... men," Gloria said, adding a little excitement to the cabby's day.

"Did you hear about that Chinese guy from the movies they're after? It's all over the news. They think he murdered that famous star actress Ruby Russell. Man, she is a beauty. Well, sad to say, was a beauty. I don't know how anybody could do that, you know, kill someone. You must be used to it, seeing dead bodies and all. Bet you've more than seen them. You probably know a lot of dirt about it, yeah?"

"We can't divulge anything about our work," Gloria said, nudging Lester.

Lester rolled his eyes and smiled.

"Here we are Agents, Fifty United Nations Plaza. That'll be $2.40. I hope you enjoyed your ride. I hope you catch the bastard."

Lester handed him three dollars. "Keep it. Good luck to you with your cab."

"Oh, this? This isn't my cab. I'm just driving until I get into the movies. I'm an actor," the cabbie said.

Gloria looked at Lester and shrugged.

"Well, look who showed up. The P.I. and ...?"

"Gloria Saville, my assistant," Lester said with a smile.

"Nothing funny, Detective," said the trim young man in a dark suit and polished shoes.

"Not detective per se any longer, Agent. Private Investigators," Lester said proudly.

"Well, Mr. Caine, once a detective, always a detective in my book," he answered. "I'm Agent Watson. I know who you are and why you're in San Francisco. It's a good thing you came in on your own, and we didn't have to hunt you down. Now, tell me what you know about Lei Chang." He gave Lester the fish-eyed stare.

"Well, Agent Watson," Gloria began, but Watson interrupted her, holding his hand up.

"I want to hear from Detective Caine," he said, ignoring Gloria.

"Easy, Agent. She's a licensed P.I., and a former Army Intelligence Officer. She's capable of answering questions you may have. We are a team. You need to know that. She had my back during our chase with Mr. Chang."

Gloria got warm and tingly and wet, hearing Lester defend her. A quick reminder of what took place together in the shower after Helen Tilly left their room added to her sexual heat. The memory of warm water cascading over their naked bodies, the feel of his hands as he lathered soap over her body, backing her against the tile, and how they ....

"Miss Saville. Are you alright? You look a little flushed," Agent Watson said, seeing Gloria stare at nothing.

"Huh? Oh, yes. I'm fine, Agent, Thank you."

"Okay. Lay it on me. Either of you."

"We were staking out Yu Yīng's place and tracking her movements," Gloria started, reverting to her role as a seasoned investigator and not a pretty accessory for Lester.

"And..."

"And we knew Chang forced Yu Yīng to hide him," Lester added.

"How? How do you know that?"

"She works at a laundry, and we witnessed her taking a package of men's shirts from the shelf and carrying the package out of the store. That's all. She is not married and doesn't have a boyfriend. Simple," Gloria said.

Agent Watson reached for the intercom. "Get the agents on the Chang stakeout in here as soon as you can," he shouted. "Why the Hell didn't they pick up on that and you did? Some heads are going to roll." Watson slammed the speaker. "Go on."

"We tailed her to her place, stopped her at her door, and she tried to convince us he left. All hell broke loose. He was there. We ran after him up to the roof. He fired a few rounds, I returned fire, and he was gone. Just like that," Lester said, snapping his fingers.

"Just like that," Agent Watson said, mimicking Lester's finger snap.

"Yes, sir, just like that," Gloria repeated with a touch of sarcasm, snapping her fingers, and staring him in the eye.

"So, your man got away? That's too bad, Mr. Caine, and you, too, Miss Saville. It is Miss Saville, am I correct?" Watson returned the sarcasm.

"It is, Agent Watson," Gloria bantered, with a bit of insolence.

"So, where do we stand? There is nothing more to tell. Can we go now?" Lester asked.

"Are you staying at the..." hesitating and picking up a piece of paper ... "The Hollywood Hotel?"

"Yes, we are," Lester said.

"Okay. We'll be in touch if necessary. If you make plans to leave. Please notify us.

"Of course, Agent Watson," Gloria said, extending her hand to shake his. *I've chewed up and spit out men like you in the Army. I know your kind.*

CHAPTER

THIRTY-ONE

The Abracadabra Studios and Frenchie arranged for Lester and Gloria to have a car at their disposal after the Chinatown incident. They had to get Lei Chang off the streets and behind bars. He had become a dangerous and desperate, wanted man. No one could predict what he would do to escape capture. The studio executives and their public relations people agreed any more shootouts or destruction of property would not be good for the box office ticket sales. The press was all over this, sending it over the wires and coming across the Teletype daily like a poison pen.

The Abracadabra Studio President, Roger Puglia, along with Jonathan Deinhart, President of Quarter Moon Productions, were good gatekeepers, adept at keeping the stockholders happy and at arm's length, like a savvy Mom with an eye on the kids in the back seat in the rearview mirror yet close enough to reach back and smack them if they needed discipline. The studio heads needed Lei Chang to be disciplined and quickly. Puglia and Deinhart were masters at breaking box office record earnings. They spun the adverse newspaper headlines to their advantage, using clips of Ruby Russell and her stunt man, Lei Chang, in previous movies.

Banners blasted the message, *"WANTED FOR RUBY'S MURDER. REWARD AWAITS YOU,"* above Chang's photo on billboards, city buses, newspapers, and called in markers from Look, Good Housekeeping, Life, Harpers, The Saturday Review, Time, Ladies' Home Journal, and The New York Times magazines. Each magazine had both Ruby Russell's and Lei Chang's photos on the front cover.

To reduce the studios' share of volatility and discouraging speculator trading and jumping ship, they convinced the Board of Directors to approve a reverse stock split because of the negative press so the Exchange would not delist the security and the studios go into bankruptcy. This move made the corporate stock proportionally more valuable, increasing the price per share. The public ate it up. Their stock prices soared. The movie houses around the world opened their doors seven days a week for two daily showings of Ruby's movies. The reporters clamored to interview the two financial geniuses, Roger Pugllia and Jonathan Deinhart.

DAY 33
THE ABRACADABRA STUDIOS

Lester and Gloria met Frenchie in the back lot, where the security guard had evicted Lester and Lizzy Thomson from Ruby Russell's trailer.

"What do you expect to find here?" Frenchie asked with raised eyebrows.

"Did the police search here?" Gloria asked.

"No, I would have known. It is studio protocol for an escort through the lot. And if it was for Ruby's trailer, it would be me."

"And if you were in Palm Beach?" Lester asked.

"I don't see any reason anyone would require access to her trailer. Ruby would be with me in Palm Beach.

We were always together. If need be, one of my studio assistants would be available." Frenchie stated.

BANG–BANG–BANG

"Miss Dubois, is that you in there?" a voice shouted.

"Yes, Clarence," Frenchie said, opening the door.

"Everything okay in here? Hey, don't I know you?" He pointed toward Lester. "You look familiar."

"I have one of those familiar faces," Lester said, turning away. "This is my first time here."

"Alright, Miss Dubois. I'll be around if you need me," Clarence reassured her.

Lester smirked. "Hmm."

"What?" Frenchie asked.

"How many people have access to this trailer?" Gloria said.

"Me and my studio assistant. No one else. Security monitors these trailers twenty-four hours a day and all of them have state-of-the-art locks, Gloria. These aren't tents in the jungles of Burma."

How the hell did Lizzy Thomson get keys? Lester wondered.

Lester and Gloria gave the dressing trailer a thorough going over, and they drew a blank. They found nothing that would advance their investigation. Another dead end.

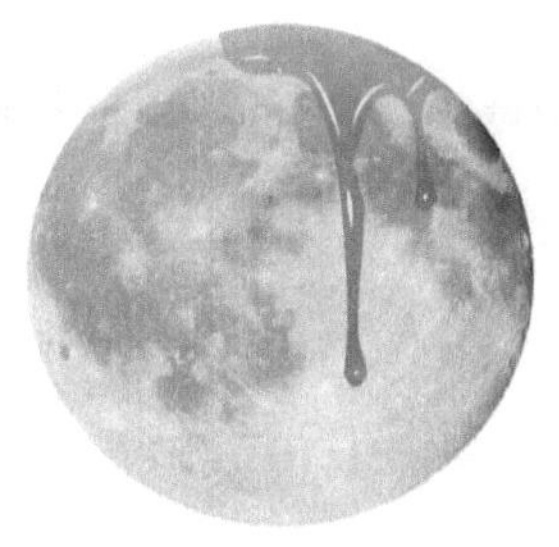

THIRTY-TWO

They hightailed it back to Chinatown. The SFPD and the FBI staked out Yu Yīng's place.

"Looks like we're in third place here, Lester. There's the fake repair truck with the FBI and the cops are walking around like they're sightseeing and shopping," Gloria said. "And I'm not in disguise. They could recognize us."

"Well, let's just show some balls and go right to her apartment. What are they going to do, stop us? That'll blow their stakeout."

"She's not so ignorant, Lester. She can't be a porcelain China doll that just stares and looks straight ahead. Yu

Yīng has to know she's being watched or may really try to help Chang escape."

"You just may be on to something. And you're a doll yourself, Gloria. Let's get this."

They wrangled their way past the law's centurion guards without being identified by the surveillance teams. They entered the building and quietly climbed the stairwell with their weapons close, turning … bending … crouching … and listening with each step for what might spring at them.

"Miss Yīng? It's Immigration. Open the door or we'll break it open," Lester said.

"I have paper. What you want? You go."

"We no go, Miss Ying. Open the door or we will…" Gloria stopped as the door slowly opened.

Glora held up her Private Investigation badge together with her P.I. license, giving the appearance of government authority.

"You here long time. You chase…" and stopped short before she blurted out Lei's name.

"You must come with us," Gloria said as she quickly handcuffed Yu's hands behind her back.

"I do nothing wrong. Where we go? I show you paper," she said, her voice quaking with nerves.

"Where are they?" Gloria asked.

"In room. Behind honorable mother and father."

In 1943, The Chinese Exclusion Act was repealed. During WWII, China became a key ally. The United States government loosened restrictions, allowing the Chinese to live and work in the U.S.

Gloria spotted a photo standing atop the simple three drawer bureau. With Yu by her side, Gloria picked up the photo and turned it over. There were Yu Yīng's immigration documents. Her papers were authentic—signed, sealed and delivered.

"Take her. Let's get out of here. Down the back stairwell to the car," Lester said.

"Stop, Lester. Do you see what I see?"

"What? He's not here. He comes, has a cup of tea, takes her money, and leaves via the roof like he lost us," Lester said.

"I do no wrong. Where we go? No, no. That tea with friend. She comes. We have China tea. All good. Now you go. Lei no here since you chase. He no come. He stupid man. Go back to China."

"Not yet. You come with us," Gloria said, grabbing Yu's arm to lead her out.

Gloria looked at Lester with eyebrows raised. "So?"

"Hotel. You sit in the back with her. I'll drive."

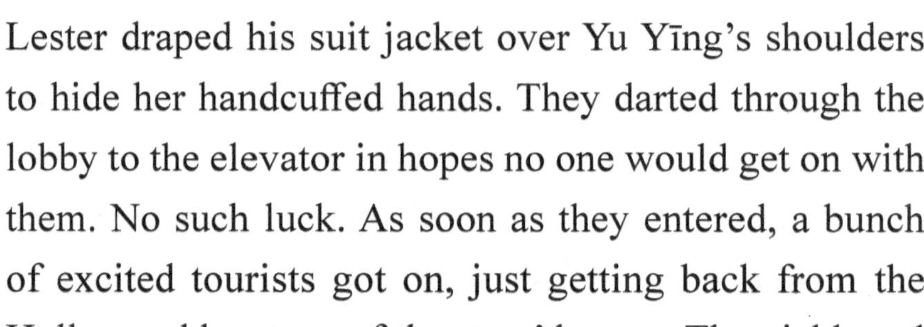

Lester draped his suit jacket over Yu Yīng's shoulders to hide her handcuffed hands. They darted through the lobby to the elevator in hopes no one would get on with them. No such luck. As soon as they entered, a bunch of excited tourists got on, just getting back from the Hollywood bus tour of the stars' homes. They jabbered about the places they saw.

Gloria stood in front of Yu, stepping backward to pin her against the elevator wall. Lester blocked Yu's other side. The elevator stopped. They each had Yu's arm and pushed through the crowd without a scrimmage. No one noticed. They were too starstruck and enchanted by Hollywood.

CHAPTER

THIRTY-THREE

Gloria released the cuffs on Yu.

"Me here. Now what you want? I have nothing."

"Yu, we know you are helping Lei. You must know where he is. He comes to you for money. He can't live with no money," Lester said.

"No. He do nothing. He no hurt lady. He go back China."

"How do you know he went back to China?" Gloria asked.

"He say. Must go. He takes money. He brother. Chinese people help family. No question. Just do."

"How is he going?" Gloria asked, knowing he couldn't board a plane.

"Yu, Lei has to have help. Is he going by boat?" Lester said.

"Me no know. Just take money, go. I work hard. Long, long time me here. I like. Me no go back to China. No good. Now I start again. Me go now."

"Soon, Yu. You can go soon. First, we must find where Lei is hiding. He will get hurt if we don't find him. The police want to hurt Lei. We want to help him. You help us and we help you and Lei," Lester said.

"Me no need help. Know nothing. Me do nothing."

"Oh, yes, you have. You gave Lei money to escape. That means you helped a fugitive to escape. You can go to prison. We are going now," Lester said.

"You go now."

"No, you are going to jail," Gloria said.

"Where I go if I tell you?"

"If we see Lei is where you tell us, you go home," Lester said.

"You go where I tell you. Lei, stupid man. He no good. He steal my money."

Gloria wrote what Yu told her where Lei was and then took her to the bathroom.

"Sit here." Lifting the toilet seat, she cuffed one hand to the sink. "We'll be back. If we find Lei, you can go home."

"Hang that Do Not Disturb sign on the door, and lock it," Lester said. "If housekeeping finds Yu in the bathroom, Chang gets away and we face kidnapping charges."

They followed Yu's directions to downtown Los Angeles to the heart of the wholesale and warehouse district on Los Angeles Street. Crime and prostitution were rampant. The warehouse where Yu said they could find Lei was situated a short distance to where the railroad cars pulled in to load goods being shipped around the country. A perfect place for Lei to hide among migrant workers and for him to jump on a shipment going who knows where on the boxcars.

A large laundry service company servicing the west coast of the United States occupied the entire six stories of the building, employing hundreds of workers. All Chinese workers. Lei could fit right in. Easy for him to work. He had experience in the industry, and his background allowed him to blend.

They entered the front entrance, and the receptionist stopped them.

"May I help you?"

They heard a soft, polite voice coming from behind the high standing counter.

Lester showed Lei's photo along with his private investigator's badge.

"We're looking for this man. Where does he work? What floor?" Lester said.

"I don't recognize him. We have two hundred employees here, Detective. He could be anywhere."

Gloria thought about her comment, identifying them as detectives. *People just assumed a badge and credentials were police, usually without carefully looking at them.*

"Do you have a name?" She asked.

"We do. Lei Chang. He's probably using a different name," Gloria said.

"Well, let me look at our list. … Hmm, I don't see that name. I'm sorry, Detective. Maybe another name?" she said in a matter-of-fact manner.

"We'll just show ourselves around," Lester said.

"Go ahead, detectives," she said, dialing the phone.

"Let's move it, Gloria. She's calling someone to alert them, probably security.

They climbed the stairway. *If Lei's here, he'll make his way down the stairs, but we can't count on that. With his stunt man skills, we can only hope he won't use another escape route.* Lester thought of Lei's escape over the roof in Chinatown. As they reached the third level, dozens of workers came toward them, crowding the stairs, bumping into them. Both men and women surrounded Lester and Gloria, all talking loudly in Chinese. They were caught in their midst.

"It's a ploy, Gloria. Whoever she called,"

"They must rehearse this maneuver to help one another if need be. It's like a stampede."

They tried to press against the wall to let them pass, but there seemed to be no end to them. The crowd herded Lester and Gloria like sheep, guiding them downstairs in the same direction as the mob, escorting them to the front door. The workers stood, blocking them from coming in and going back up the stairs.

"Son of a bitch," Gloria said. "We've been had. Now we know he is or was here."

"All's not lost, Gloria. Let's drive around to the boxcars. We've got nothing to lose. He's in the wind or in the building. We'll give this to the FBI. They'll come in and upset this choreographed mob."

"Well, do you think Yu told us the truth?" Lester asked.

"Oh shit, Yu! I've got her handcuffed to the sink. We need to hightail it back to the hotel. Who knows what she might be up to?"

THIRTY-FOUR

THE HOLLYWOOD PLAZA HOTEL
LESTER AND GLORIA'S ROOM

"Lester, let's put Lei Chang aside now that we got her back to her apartment. Let's enjoy this evening. We deserve this. Twice, someone fired shots at us. We could have been killed. The laundry building incident humiliated us, and it's damaging our reputation. We've been chasing Chang for over one month," Gloria said, reaching for Lester's hand. "I'm going to freshen up. Get comfortable. Why don't you shed your tie and whatever else relaxes you? I ordered room service for us. They should be here soon. I'll be right out."

"I see your point, Gloria. This is good living. Hollywood style."

"Yeah," her word lingered, hanging, not fully revealing her full thoughts.

The California sunset painted the horizon a hue of magnificent amber. Room service delivered a full course meal to the balcony, where Lester and Gloria waited to enjoy the fillet mignon steak cooked to perfection, seared exterior and a tender, juicy pink center. The Sommelier had poured the Cabernet Sauvignon into the stemmed wine glasses and lit the candles.

"Is there anything else, Mr. Caine?

"No, thank you. Add ten percent on the bill for you."

"Yes Sir, thank you."

"You know what? Make it fifteen percent. You did a great job here."

"Thank you again, Mr. Caine. That is generous of you. Have a—"

Gloria came out of the bathroom in her white silk pajamas, interrupting him.

"Good evening," he mumbled and rushed out the door.

"Come here, Lester. Let me take off that tie," she said, loosening it and slowly sliding it from under his collar and down across his chest like the biblical snake slithered around the Garden of Eden, tempting Eve to succumb to temptation. Desire swamped her. Desire with no redemption. She led him to the table that looked like a perfect movie set with a perfect backdrop.

She pulled out his chair, then strolled to her own. His eyes kept a steady watch of her slow saunter, like a cat purring and rubbing along your leg with those slinky pajamas that clung to her body. Lester stared, appreciating her beauty again, the sixth or seventh time. He couldn't really remember. She wasn't wearing anything underneath the silk. She sat. He stared. She'd left three top buttons undone. The silk draped lovingly over her breasts. Her nipples puckered. She speared a piece of steak with her fork, leaned forward and offered it to him, teasing him as the top of her pajamas gaped, exposing her breasts. He had never seen her like this with a softness. She leaned back and lifted her wineglass.

"Per cento anni. It means for one-hundred years, Lester."

"Per cento anni," he repeated to the clink of glasses ringing together.

Lester remembered the feel and curves of her smooth, tawny skin embracing her sweet scent.

Gloria clearly remembered the firmness of his embrace, and yet this was a new side to her feeling. She felt the expression to 'make love' was a bit maudlin. 'Having sex' was more fitting and 'fucking' was arousing. This time, she wanted all three.

Lester got up, took her by the hand, and led her to the bedroom.

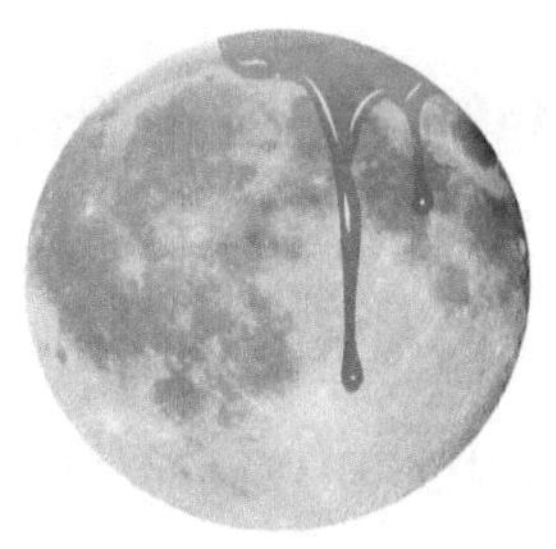

CHAPTER

THIRTY-FIVE

A loud knock on their hotel room door, more like pounding, roused Lester.

"Mr. Caine, open the door. It's the San Francisco Police. We need to speak to you. NOW! This can't wait. Mr. Caine. Open the door or I'll have the hotel manager open it."

"I'm coming, I'm coming. I'm here," Lester said, tying his robe as he walked to the door. He couldn't decide what was more annoying, the pounding on the door or the boisterous words on the other side.

"What's all the hullabaloo?" Gloria asked from the bedroom door.

"Mr. Caine. ... Ma'am. I know Miss Dubois hired you to find Miss Russell's murderer."

"Well, Detective, the Abracadabra Studios and Quarter Moon Productions really hired us. They're footing the tab. What does that have to do with the price of tomatoes?"

"What tomatoes?" he asked

"Never mind. The point is, what does who hired us, who's paying, and what they're paying for have to do with your wake-up call?" Gloria asked.

"Your client, Miss Dubois, is missing."

"She's not our client. She's the go-between, Detective. What do you mean, she's missing?" Lester said.

"She's missing. Mr. Puglia called us. They can't reach her anywhere. They've sent their security people to Miss Russell's home in Topanga. The housekeeper said Miss Dubois packed a bag and left no word for anyone. The staff in Palm Beach have not heard from her. Seems really strange that both Miss Dubois and Mr. Chang are missing, and we just found out that Miss Yu Yīng, Chang's sister, is gone too. My men went to her apartment, and it's empty. The laundry where she worked said she got her pay for the week and hasn't been seen. This is not the norm, all three in the wind. Don't you agree, Mr. Caine?"

"I do, Detective, I do. Gloria?" Lester turned to her, shifting his eyes toward the detective, signaling her to agree and not get into a fracas with him.

"Oh, my God! Of course. We'll get dressed, Detective, and come down to the Precinct, if that's okay with you. Maybe we can put our heads together and share information. Maybe we'll figure out what's going on here."

"We have a car. Give us an hour," Lester said.

"One hour. Anything more and my men will come and escort you. Do I make myself clear?"

"We got it, Detective. We're on your side, remember?" Gloria said. "We want Chang as bad as you and we want to know where Miss Dubois is and why Yu Ying is not around too. So, leave and we can get ready," Gloria said, shooing them out like a farmer's wife with chickens in her garden.

"Gloria, what the hell is happening here? Are you thinking what I'm thinking?"

"Beat me, daddy, eight to the bar," she exclaimed.

CHAPTER

THIRTY-SIX

| SAN FRANCISCO POLICE HEADQUARTERS.

They arrived at police headquarters before the police posse came knocking on their hotel door again.

"Glad you're able to join us," said the Police Lieutenant with a sneer.

"We want to get to the bottom of this too. I've contacted the studios, spoke to Mr. Puglia, and he checked with Mr. Deinhart. We have a new circumstance that just came to our attention. We're bringing it to you as well, so we're all on the same page. I contacted the Palm Beach Police Lieutenant just before we came here."

"Okay, Mr. Caine, let's have it.".

"Miss Russell's studio account is shy one million dollars. Miss Dubois assured us there was nothing wrong with Ruby's finances or she would have known," Lester said.

"One million!" he exclaimed with a whistle.

"So, Lieutenant, it appears—.

"It means," the Lieutenant interrupted Gloria, "that Miss Dubois embezzled $1,000,000. With all the focus on Mr. Chang, she thought the money would not be missed, or at least not so soon. So, is she in this alone or are Miss Dubois, Chang, and Chang's sister, Yu Ying, in this together? According to Miss Dubois's Topanga house staff, she disappeared right around the time you were shot at, changing the focus and putting a different angle on this investigation."

"Lieutenant, if all three are in this together, Miss Dubois and Chang's sister can slip away. Chang has an All-Points Bulletin out on him. We've alerted the airports and train stations. His picture is plastered all over the media and a high-dollar reward has been offered. He can only get out by private plane or boat. He's not Houdini," Lester said.

"We know, Mr. Caine. Our phone lines are lit up like a Christmas tree, with callers claiming they know where Lei Chang is hiding. We check every lead, no matter how ridiculous. They are all dead ends, but they're willing to chance that Chang is where they say and they will get a big payday. We've dealt with this before. It cost the city thousands of dollars, in manpower," the Lieutenant said.

"Yes, Lieutenant, but you never know what a tip could yield. Am I correct?" Gloria stated.

"You are, Ma'am,"

"It's Gloria Saville, Lieutenant. I am a licensed investigator, along with Mr. Caine."

"Well..." hesitating, "Mrs. Saville, I see. Thank you for that clarification."

"Miss, Miss Saville, Lieutenant."

"I stand corrected. Forgive me. Now that we cleared that up. Ah, ahem," clearing his throat. "Let's see what we can do together to get all three suspects in one place."

"Lieutenant, we're here; we're on-board. We don't enjoy being shot at or hung out to dry. Let's get to work," Lester said.

"My men are on a rotation for the docks and the trains. All the cab companies are on notice as well with his photo in each cab," the Lieutenant said.

"We had a lead from his sister, who led us to where he was working to pick up some extra money. A laundering company," Lester said.

"Probably one over in the warehouse district, Los Angeles Street. If that's true, he could have hopped a freight train to anywhere. That's one avenue we can't keep up with. He could jump from train to train to train all the way to Timbuktu."

"Let's hope not, Lieutenant. In the meantime, your boys in blue can check the airlines and trains for Amélie Dubois. She uses Frenchie as well. Yu Yīng should be easy to recognize. They could travel separate and have plans to meet up later," Gloria said.

"If they're all in on this one million dollar embezzlement, I don't think either Chang or his sister will be too far from Miss Dubois," said the Lieutenant.

"Could very well be, Lieutenant. We are going back to the studios and snoop around a bit. I want to see if we can pick up a paper trail where the money might be. You'll be the first to know if we find anything," Lester said.

"In the meantime, Lieutenant, can you get a search warrant for the laundry premises?" Gloria asked. "We can go in and give it a good going over. They bamboozled us when we went there on our lead. They all stuck together, creating a crowd, and literally pushed us down the stairs and into the street. Then they blocked us from re-entering,"

"Ah. Sure. I got it, Miss Saville. You want us to toss the place? Sort of eye for an eye? The Old Testament thing, I like the way you think. Hang on to her, Caine, You've got a good one here," the Lieutenant responded. "I can relate. Why not?"

"Well, Lester, here's the *Knights of Swords Card* that Pamela turned over—cheating in order to do harm."

"Pamela is ... is ..."

"What?"

"Spot on with her Tarot readings."

"Sure as shit, Lester. I may have to take her up on learning how to read the tarot cards."

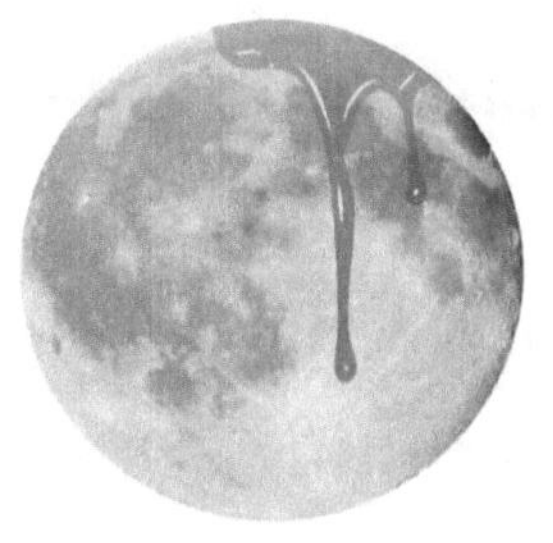

THIRTY-SEVEN

ABRACADABRA STUDIOS
THE ACCOUNTING DEPARTMENT

"Go right in Mr. Caine, Miss Saville. They are expecting you," said the receptionist.

"What is it you wanted to look at, Mr. Caine, Miss Saville?" asked the chief studio accountant.

"Well, to start, how was Miss Dubois able to get $1,000,000 out of Miss Russell's account with no one asking where it was going and to whom?"

"Well, we've tracked it. There's no question our records show it embezzled. Let me show you. See. It's tied to an investment. Over a period of time, Miss Russell helped finance a project in Miami with other investors, including her then husband, John Arthur."

"That investment was almost a loss. They just about broke even from what her divorce attorney's husband told us. Mr. Thomson was the developer. Isn't that right, Gloria?" Lester said.

"It is," she answered.

"So, they, or I should say Miss Dubois, still cut checks to these vendors. The description of these entries was for that project, but the money was deposited in another account. The money should have linked to invoices for the real estate investment and for her managing fees," said the accountant. "Miss Dubois was withdrawing checks made out to a bogus company. As we see, a fake company with fake invoices. The fake or shell company was Miss Dubois's company. Then she took the money, deposited it into that shell company and put it in accounts somewhere offshore, as we found out during our audit."

"Why did you investigate Miss Russell's accounts?" Gloria asked.

"It's a formality, Miss Saville. We contract with an outside accounting firm to audit all our stars' accounts who have contracts with us. It's done annually. One of the most common warning signs in bookkeeping fraud is inconsistent or missing documentation. If you notice discrepancies in invoices, receipts, or bank statements such as large payments to unfamiliar vendors or excessive cash withdrawals.”

“Bookkeepers use a double entry system, recording every transaction in two accounts: a debit to one and a credit to another. For example, when a business takes out a $5,000 loan, we debit the cash (asset) account $5,000 and credit the outstanding debt (liability) account $5,000. This means cash and outstanding debt are now increased by the same amount. Miss Dubois failed to do that. Instead, she created fake invoices to offset the debt and paid to her fake account.”

“So, Miss Dubois had plenty of time knowing that you only audit once a year,” Gloria said.

“Yes, and because of this, we now audit quarterly.”

“Do you know the offshore location where the money landed?” Lester asked.

“Sadly, yes.”

“I don’t get it, why sadly? If you know where it is, why is that sad?” Gloria asked.

“Because I assume it’s in a Swiss numbered bank account,” Lester said. “Am I right?”

“You are correct, Mr. Caine. And there is nothing we can do to find it. It would be impossible to follow the money, as you say in police jargon,”

“Well, $1,000,000 is a damn good pay day even if it is doled out six ways to Sunday,” Lester said.

"You are so right, Mr. Caine," he answered with chagrin.

"Thank you. We'll get out of your hair," Lester said, standing.

"Gloria. I'm thinking that Chang is right under our noses."

"What do you mean, Lester? You don't think he's in the wind?"

"Frenchie and Yu Yīng may be, but I think Chang is close by. Think about this. He knows he has no way out except by hopping train to train to train. Then what? To Canada or Mexico. He would need resources and lots of cash, which we know he does not have. Amélie Dubois has that money in Switzerland. Chang can't get it, and Yu will not leave her side. If Frenchie and Yu are on their way to Europe, Chang wants his cut off the scratch."

"And that's a lot to scratch any itch, any place, any time. You're right. He has to jump a freighter or a ship. The SFPD said they have the docks covered. It could be a private plane," Gloria said.

"It must be. So, where would you hide now that Yu's place was scoured and is empty? No one's going back there to look again. The SFPD and the FBI wrote that off. I didn't," Lester said.

"Let's get a move on," Gloria answered, eager for action.

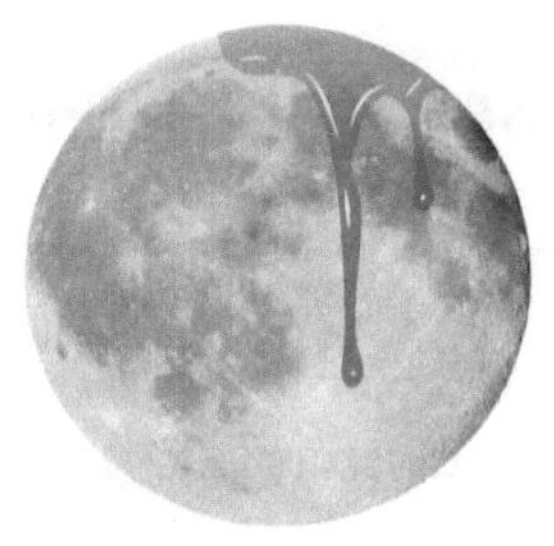

THIRTY-EIGHT

They cautiously climbed the stairwell to Yu Yīng's abandoned apartment. The leftover smells waft in the hallway, the powerful bouquet of a strong pungent scent of ginger and garlic with an underlying aroma of earthy mushrooms and root vegetables. It was the essence of Chinese cooking that dispelled the poverty lurking behind every apartment door.

"Jesus, Lester, that smell is making me hungry. You know how I like Chinese takeout."

"Let's just concentrate on why we're here right now."

"If he is, he's not stupid. He knows SFPD and the FBI wouldn't be back here, and it gives him some time," Gloria said.

"Quiet," Lester said, placing his fingers to his lips.

They took each stair step slowly, listening after each one. Lester looking up and Gloria looking down to be sure they covered each other.

Lester placed his ear to the door, listened carefully, hoping no one would come out of their apartment and start yelling a warning in their native language. He turned toward Gloria, nodding two times. He's in there. Their background and experience had taught them how to break a door open. No fancy martial arts move. Just military and law enforcement training. Lester surveyed the flimsy wooden door. No hinges, which meant the door swung in as he remembered. He knew the weakest part of the door—to the right of the lock near the frame. They both knew the imminent response of whoever was behind the door. Their guns drawn, Lester signed to Gloria. He held up three fingers to count down and bust through the door. Three! … Two! … One!

Lester's kick broke the door lock. The door swung ajar, and they flattened themselves against the paper-thin wall. And there it was…

BLAM! BLAM!

"Only two shots," Gloria said. "That's stingy of him. I thought we were worth more."

They rushed in. Chang turned and fired over his shoulder, without aiming, running up the fire escape again, creating tension and anxiety among the guests. The loud sonic boom made their ears ring. Bullets whizzed by, pinging off the stove, and ricochetting erratically.

"Down the back stairs, c'mon," Lester yelled. "We've got to get to the street."

They spilled onto the sidewalk with guns drawn, yelling, **"move–move–move, detectives!"** They shoved people out of the way, uncaring who fell into the delivery boxes of fresh produce left curbside. Lester couldn't identify himself as a cop.

"I see him," Gloria yelled. "To your left, follow the roofline."

Chang fired aimlessly downward. Chaos occurred exactly as he wanted. Crowds of tourists, workers, and residents screamed, pushed, ran, scrambling in every direction, causing confusion. Lester and Gloria got caught in the middle of a stampede. No-one knew what was happening. The gunfire scattered them like roaches in a dark place when a light came on.

Incredibly, Chang leaped, clearing the alley between the two buildings with ease. He turned and saluted them his middle finger. Then he crouched and ran. Just like the last time, he was gone.

"We had him. Where'd he go?" Gloria said.

"He must be in that building where he dropped onto the roof. Let's get in there," Lester said.

"I'm right behind you,"

They ran down the alley looking for a way in. There! A door swung open, hitting Gloria's arm, breaking her grip on her gun. It dropped to the ground. She looked up and Chang was looking down at her. He lifted his gun to her head.

BAM!

One shot. That's all it took. Chang fell to his knees, dropped his gun, and fell to the ground. He groaned, holding his stomach. Lester ran to Gloria.

"Gloria, are you okay?"

"That fucker almost had me, Lester. Thank you. You saved my life. I owe you now, big time."

Lester took a hankie and pressed Chang's stomach.

"You'll live, Chang," Lester said. "It's not so bad. The slug hit your side. You hear the sirens? They're coming for you."

"Lucky me. Ha."

"Lei Chang, you know you're going to prison, possibly face the electric chair. Why don't you tell me where Amélie Dubois and your sister Yu Yīng are?"

"I do not know what you're talking about, Caine. I have done nothing wrong."

"You'll get the death penalty for the murder of Ruby Russell. You'll never stand trial for the attempted murder of me and Miss Saville, because Ruby's murder will be the first trial. The jury will convict you and the judge will sentence you to death. The second trial for attempted murder will follow. They will convict you of that, but the sentence is meaningless because you won't survive to serve it. They will fry you like a flounder in deep, hot oil."

"Go fuck yourself, Caine. I did not kill Ruby."

THIRTY-NINE

FRANKLIN HOSPITAL
NOE STREET, SAN FRANCISCO
THIRD FLOOR, ROOM 8

The SFPD swarmed the hospital as if the queen bee in her hive was under attack. From the moment they wheeled Lei Chang in from the emergency room, through surgery, recovery, and to his private room, police officers guarded the entrances, exits, and hallway to his room. They posted a sign on the door to his room.

Private-No Visitors

Lester thought the sign odd. *Who the hell would come to visit him?*

"Hello Lieutenant," Lester said.

"Ah, Mr. Caine. I wish I could address you properly as a detective. You and your associate did good work, superb. Now the fun begins. You know I have to ask you and Miss Saville for your guns and P.I. licenses. Just a formality. I'm sure it's not your first shooting. I'll get it back to you as soon as I can. Maybe two days. I'll push it. It was a good shoot. We have his gun."

"Yes, Lieutenant, not our first, and it was by the book. We know the drill. Appreciate their swift return. Thanks."

"We'll forego the blood and alcohol test on you both. And from what I'm told, it's impossible to get any witnesses from the scene because of the commotion Mr. Chang caused. Ah, here comes the surgeon now."

"Here's the bullet you requested, Lieutenant. Mr. Chang is lucky to be alive. An inch either way, and that slug would have ripped through some vital organs. He'll be fine. He should be awake in a few hours and able to answer questions. Good luck," he said.

"Thanks, Doc. I appreciate ..." and stopped as the surgeon walked away to attend to more important matters.

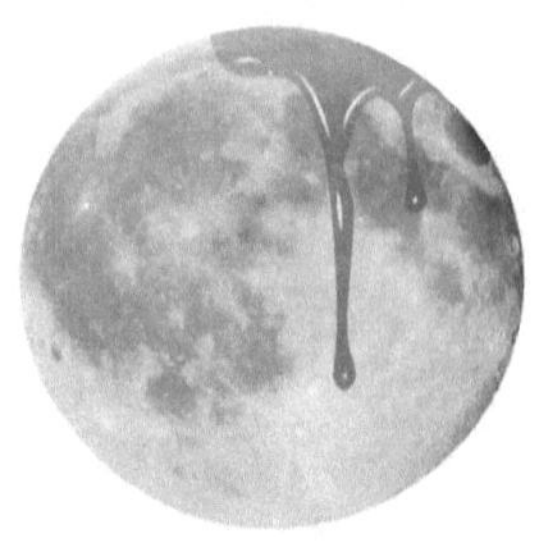

CHAPTER

FORTY

Lester and Gloria flew back to Los Angeles from Palm Beach after catching up on agency work they had left behind while pursuing Lei Chang. They still had to find Amélie Dubois and Yu Yīng, who were reaping the benefits of Amélie's $1,000,000 embezzlement. Lester Caine Investigations was still under contract with Abracadabra Studios and Quarter Moon Productions.

Mr. Puglia and Mr. Deinhart were rigorously seeking the conviction of Lei Chang for the murder of their box office star, Ruby Russell. The heinous act would cost them millions in lost future revenues. Movie houses around the world were clamoring for the re-release of Ruby's movies. The public could not get enough of her films, but her fame would fade with time when no new properties were available. Studio executives knew a narrow window of opportunity existed to cash in on the public fervor before archiving the present films, perhaps eventually losing them in some dusty studio warehouse. They had no Ruby Russell prospect in the studios' futures.

The extradition papers for transporting Chang were good to go. So was he. Ruby Russell's murder occurred in Palm Beach. Chang had to be tried there. Lester, Gloria and Chang had a police escort to the L.A. Airport, through the gate and onto the tarmac where a private plane waited, the arrangements made by the studios.

"Lester, I'm glad this isn't a commercial flight. I've done a few of these extraditions when I was an Army Intelligence Officer. We had Military Police escorts. This cuts our chances of things going awry," she said.

"I agree, don't you, Mr. Chang?" Lester asked with obvious sarcasm.

"What the hell can I do, handcuffed? And, I'm still sore and mending. The Doc said maybe another three weeks would have been better for me to fully mend. If I wasn't afraid of re-injuring myself or my hands were free, I'd show you, Caine."

"What? You want a repeat performance of our dance at Ruby's mansion in Palm Beach? Ah, stop flappin' your lips. That's just a stall. The Doc said you were fine to travel, and I say you'll be in good health by the time they fish fry you."

"Fuck you, Caine. You too, you bitch," looking at Gloria.

"Be a lady, Gloria. Settle down. Let me," Lester said, bouncing Chang's head into the back of the seat he was staring at. Reading Gloria, he knew she was about to belt him one.

"Oh, fuck. That's right. You're a big man with me all cuffed up and not able to defend myself."

Lester grabbed the back of Chang's head again.

"Wait, Lester. My turn," Gloria said.

"Okay, I get it. I won't say anything. I got the message," Chang said.

"You'll have your day in court, fry fish-boy." Gloria said, smirking.

"Fuck you too," Chang said.

"My turn." Gloria knocked Chang's head against the seat. "Ah, that's better."

"Feeling better, Gloria, now that's out of your system?" Lester asked.

"Why, thank you, Lester. I do. How do you feel, Mr. Chang? Another?" she asked.

"No, I'm good," he said, panting. "I'm good. I will never tell you where Frenchie and Yu are. Frenchie and I … I owe her. She saved me from Fat Chow, Boss of Chinese Pai Gow gambling in Chinatown. Look," Chang held up his hand. "He cut off the tip of my pinky finger. He said that was just a warning. It almost ruined my career. Frenchie promised to pay him. We planned to spend the rest of our lives together … somewhere you'd never find us. Yu was paying Fat Chow, too, to hold him off. Yu's not as dumb as she makes herself out. They planned the whole thing. Frenchie's real smart. She had to kill Ruby before she discovered the money in the studio account was gone. She couldn't collect Ruby's life insurance, so she embezzled money."

"Why murder her? Wouldn't she help you?" Gloria asked.

"Are you kidding? Ruby was a ruthless, mean bitch. She put on an act on and off screen for the public. Her staff and crew hated her. She would lash out over nothing. She even slapped her make-up artist, had her fired, for not getting her face made up on time. Frenchie is living the life now. But you, Caine. You got in the way. You … I'll take the hit. I killed Ruby for Frenchie. I'll fry for her."

"Ah, ain't love grand? True love, not like in the movies," Gloria snickered.

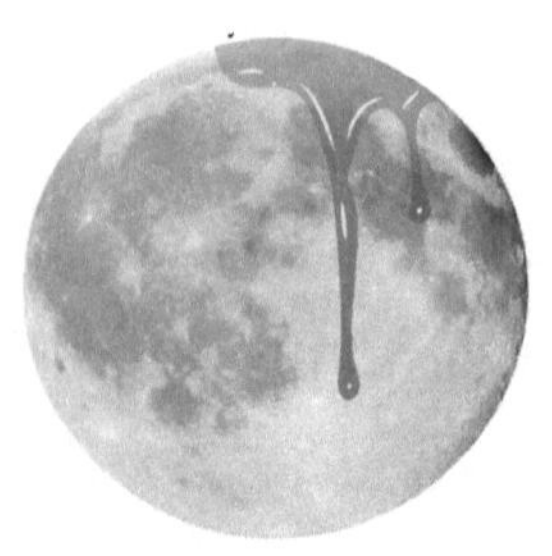

CHAPTER

FORTY-ONE

The Grand Jury delivered an indictment of Lei Chang. He now stood before the judge at a pre-trial hearing. He pleaded not guilty, and the court appointed a Public Defender to represent him.

The Palm Beach County District Attorney requested the judge deny bail for Mr. Chang on the grounds he fled in violation of the Palm Beach Police Department's admonition. Further, he attempted to flee the country. The prosecution considers Lei Chang a flight risk. In addition, attempted murder charges are pending against Lei Chang in connection with the violent pursuit and his capture by the two private investigators, Lester Caine and Gloria Saville. The D.A. requested Lei Chang surrender his passport.

The P.D. argued that Mr. Chang was born in this country, is an American citizen, has worked in the highly regarded entertainment industry everyone loves and that provides an escape from reality … motion pictures. Mr. Chang was a stuntman in Ruby Russell's movies and her security advisor. He had no motive to murder her and has not profited from her demise. She was his bread and butter and had employed Mr. Chang for years.

The D.A. argued Mr. Chang was not a United States citizen. He contended Mr. Chang could not produce a United States birth certificate and Miss Russell employed him on a work visa. Apparently, Mr. Chang was in the United States long before the repeal of the Chinese Exclusion Act allowing Asians, Philippines, and Indians to work in the United States. No one but Mr. Chang knows when or how he arrived in this country.

His Honor agreed with the prosecution and denied bail. Mr. Chang would remain a guest of Palm Beach County through the jurisprudence process and ultimate decision.

The P.D. requested a speedy trial date. "Your Honor, the Defendant requests that the court grant his constitutional right to a speedy trial."

"In the United States, the right to a speedy trial is more than a legal concept," the Judge said. "It's a fundamental constitutional right. This crucial provision ensures the proceedings do not subject Mr. Chang to unnecessary delays and safeguards him against potential government abuse of power. In this country, Mr. Chang, you are innocent until proven guilty. I will not have a denial of a speedy trial used to provide the basis of an appeal. Do we all understand this?" He looked directly at the D.A. "Are there any objections?"

If anyone had political ambitions, this case could make or break careers. The judge recognized this, and the attorneys of record knew it. Because of the prominence of the deceased, the subsequent publicity and interest, legal scholars, reporters and Miss Russell's fans would discuss and analyze every piece of evidence, argument, rebuttal, and ruling *ad nauseum.* Errors would be magnified.

"No, Your Honor. We have no objections. If the defense feels they are ready for trial, the State of Florida is ready."

"Good. We will now set the calendar."

Voir dire, interviewing and questioning potential jurors by the prosecuting and defense attorneys, and the judge, had taken days. Although twelve jurors and three alternate jurors were required, the Clerk of the Court assembled a panel of three times that number of Mr. Chang's so-called peers from which to choose. The jurors were of supreme importance in any trial, but crucial in a murder trial. Potential bias or prejudice must be identified and assessed for or against the defendant. The burden of proof whether Lei Chang was guilty of murdering Ruby Russell lay with the State. Although it appeared an open and shut case, it might not be that simple.

As the arresting detective, Lester had been called to testify in many murder trials over his twenty-five years with the New York City Police Department. He knew all too well that it only took one person on the jury panel to cause a hung jury. One opinionated person could convince enough jurors to deliver a not guilty verdict.

FORTY-TWO

| THE TRIAL

"All rise," the Bailiff instructed. "The Honorable Henry Wadsworth presiding." Judge Wadsworth's mother, a poet laureate, had named him in part for Henry Wadsworth Longfellow.

The white-haired, deeply tanned man in the black robes of a judge entered from a door in the front of the room. His law clerk trailed behind. His unimposing figure belied the importance of his role. Taking his seat, he swiveled in his chair, his gaze sweeping over the players in this judicial play, then rapped the gavel.

"This Court is now in session."

His Honor acknowledged the District Attorney and the Public Defender. The attorneys shuffled papers, and the court reporter poised over her keyboard.

The Bailiff called the case: State of Florida vs. Lei Chang, in the Circuit Court of the Fifteenth Judicial Circuit in and for Palm Beach County, Florida.

"Is the Prosecution ready?" A rhetorical question that he repeated to the Public Defender.

The Court Clerk had sworn in the Jury.

"Ladies and gentlemen of the jury …" He asked if they were comfortable, a folksy gesture, then instituted proceedings. "All jury trials begin with opening statements," he explained.

District Attorney:

"Your Honor, ladies and gentlemen of the jury. The Defendant, Lei Chang, is charged with murder in the first degree of Miss Ruby Russell. The evidence will show that the Defendant murdered Ruby Russell and then hung her by the neck, naked, from the balcony of her Palm Beach mansion. Defendant strangled Ruby Russell, then affixed a rope around her neck, and pushed Miss Russell off the balcony, trying to disguise her murder as a suicide by hanging."

Defense:

"Your Honor, ladies and gentlemen of the jury. Under the law, the Defendant, my client, is presumed innocent until proven guilty. During this trial, the prosecution will present no evidence against my client. Because there is none, only conjecture. You will come to know the truth that Mr. Chang lived in Miss Russell's house with her, her personal assistant, and the housekeeping staff. He functioned as Ruby Russell's security officer and was her loyal employee for several years. And you, the jury, must weigh all the evidence for truth because in the State of Florida, a guilty verdict carries a death sentence, not life imprisonment."

District Attorney:

Objection, Your Honor ..."

Judge:

"I'm one step ahead of you. Sustained. I instructed the jury on the law. The jury will disregard the Public Defender's last statement. The court reporter will strike the Defense's last statement from the record."

District Attorney:

"Thank you, your Honor."

Judge:

"Alright. So there are no misunderstandings, as the umpire says, and you all know I am the umpire here. I will call strikes and balls as I see them. As *I* see them. That's why I wear the robe. PLAY BALL!" He bellowed. His voice carried through the closed door and into the hallway. "The Prosecution may call its first witness."

Prosecution:

"Ladies and gentlemen, we will show Mr. Chang conspired and plotted to murder Ruby Russell. His motive was not ill treatment or dismissal, or losing a movie role, but money … simple greed. He and Miss Amélie Dubois were lovers. During their investigation, Lester Caine and Gloria Saville discovered that movie studios insured their elite stars, including Miss Russell. Miss Amélie Dubois was one beneficiary of a sizeable insurance policy, together with Abracadabra Studios and Quarter Moon Productions."

"Mr. Chang needed money to escape his sizeable gambling debt to the Chinese mobsters that ran the gambling Paigow syndicate. Mr. Chang frequently played a sophisticated 32 tile Chinese dominoes game established during the Song Dynasty. The odds usually favored the house.

"Miss Amélie Dubois would only receive one-third of the proceeds of the life insurance policy, so she embezzled

$1,000,000 from Ruby Russell's personal accounts to help Mr. Chang. Miss Dubois's whereabouts are presently unknown. Lei Chang's sister, Yu Yīng, discovered their scheme to defraud and demanded she be included or would rat them out. They planned to flee the country to escape the Chinese Paigow syndicate and Mr. Chang's debt.

"In addition, there is a Chinese belief that influenced Mr. Chang to murder Ruby Russel before sunrise. It is the belief that at the moment of death messengers take the deceased's spirit to Ch´eng Huang on the dark side of the moon for a trial before the sun can rise. Will the dead go to the Buddhist paradise to dwell with the Taoist immortals because they were good? Mr. Chang knew Ruby Russell was a good woman and would be eternally in paradise."

Witnesses were called for the prosecution. Lieutenant Walker testified to the photos of the scratch marks and the puncture wound on Lei Chang's neck and chest. The Medical Examiner's presented expert testimony on his findings and his report certifying Ruby Russell's death as a homicide. The most compelling witnesses were Alvi and his wife, Marcia, who owned Alvi's Paint and Hardware Store. Both identified Lei Chang as the person who bought the rope used to hang Miss Russell. The defense grilled them extensively. Some witnesses were on the stand for hours.

The P.D. called the Head Housekeeper, the house staff, and Mr. Gonzalez, the groundskeeper, to testify about Mr. Chang's role in the household and his relationship with Miss Russell. The dinner guests who attended Ruby Russell's last supper on the last night of her life were called, one by one, except for Amélie Dubois, who still had not been located. The District Attorney questioned and cross-examined each witness's testimony.

After days of calling witnesses and listening to testimony, the Prosecution and the Defense presented their closing arguments, and the Judge addressed the jury.

Judge to the jury:

Count One of the indictment charges the defendant with first-degree murder, violating 18 U.S. Code §1111. In order for the defendant to be found guilty of that charge, the State of Florida must prove each of the following elements beyond a reasonable doubt:

First, the defendant unlawfully killed Ruby Russell;

Second, the defendant killed Ruby Russell with malice aforethought;

Third, the killer premeditated the killing;

Fourth, the killing occurred at 10451 South Dunbar Road, Palm Beach, Florida.

To kill with malice aforethought means to kill, either deliberately and intentionally or recklessly, with an extreme disregard for human life.

Premeditation with planning or deliberation. The time needed for premeditation of a killing depends on the person and the circumstances. It must be long enough, after forming the intent to kill, for the killer to have been fully conscious of the intent and to have considered the killing. With a guilty verdict comes the penalty.

The State has presented you with the evidence at hand. You must discuss nothing from this trial with anyone except each of you in that jury room, nowhere else, not at lunch, not at dinner. I instruct you not to watch the news or read the newspapers. If you have questions, ask the Bailiff. He will be outside your door. The jury foreman, after you have chosen him or her, will deliver questions or requests to the Bailiff in writing. He will then deliver it to me. Do not hesitate to ask. No question should go unanswered. In the State of Florida, first degree murder carries the death penalty and does not require a unanimous decision. It requires a majority vote sufficient for sentencing." The Judge paused and made eye contact with each juror.

"You are dismissed to begin your deliberations. Go with God. Bailiff, escort the jurors to the jury room. Court is adjourned."

FORTY-THREE

| THE PETIT JURY

The jury comprised six men and six women. Their first task was to elect a jury foreperson. It was unusual the jury was split equally by gender.

"Let's begin," said a juror who identified herself as a schoolteacher. "What do you think about us sitting around the table as we did in court? You know, one through twelve. The alternate jurors do not take part in deliberations. I'm juror number three, so I'll sit there," she said, pointing to a chair at the table. Everyone agreed, shuffling, to select chairs by numbers.

"Now that we're all seated, let's start with juror number one. Say your name and where you work, family, hobbies. Anything you want to share."

"I'll write our qualities on the blackboard they provided us. I'm used to writing on the board." She listed their bio details for each juror on the blackboard.

1. "I'm Frank, single, and work as an orderly at St. Mary's General Hospital in West Palm Beach."

2. "I'm Harold, married for twelve years. We have a daughter. I drive a bus for the Miami Transit Company. We have 208 buses. You know, the green and tan buses some of you probably have used."

3. "I'm juror number three. My name is Cynthia, a schoolteacher for junior high school students at the George Washington High School in Ft. Lauderdale. I'm married. My husband is a welder and we have two children—a daughter and son and we have three grandchildren. I plan to retire from teaching in five years. I went from banking into teaching."

4. "I'm Ruth, not married. I work on Royal Palm Way for an Ad Agency."

5. "Hi. I'm Donald. My wife is Debbie. I am a retired banker, and we have no children. We like

to travel. I'm sure Cynthia and I could tell you a lot about banking."

6. "I am Ross. I am twice divorced. I have one son from my first marriage and I own a drugstore. I'm a pharmacist."

7. "I am number seven. Richard, known as Dick. Is seven lucky? I doubt that or I wouldn't be here serving on a murder trial. Go figure. That's all."

8. "Well, my name is Judi. I'm a legal secretary. I worked in Miami for a large law firm. I'm retired. I have two children and two grandchildren. My husband worked as an airline mechanic. That's it."

9. "Hello there. I'm Charles … Charlie, I'm known to my friends. I have a successful messenger service business in downtown Miami. I've run it for many years. I am married with five children and I'm working to put them through college."

10. "I am Donna. I am or was married. Now a widow. I have two daughters and two handsome grandsons and one beautiful granddaughter. I'm a real estate agent. I will give you my card. If any of you need my services, call me."

11. "I'm Beverly. I am divorced with three children and one grandson in college. I work at Evergreen Cemetery in Ft. Lauderdale. Many notable people

are buried. there. I live with a friend." She turned and winked at Donna.

12."Hello, everyone. I'm Karen. I am widowed. My husband was a pastry chef for one of the top restaurants in New York City—Frederico's Steak House in midtown Manhattan. Teddy Roosevelt, Albert Einstein, Frank Sinatra, Ava Gardner, and Babe Ruth were among the celebrities who enjoyed my husband's pastries. I moved to Palm Beach for the weather."

"Let's vote," said Donna, juror number ten. "I vote for Cynthia to be Madam Foreman. If you can keep a group of middle schoolers in order, you can keep us in order too."

Subdued chuckles followed her pithy suggestion.

"I second that and vote for Cynthia," Beverly, Juror number eleven, said.

Everyone agreed, relieved to pass on the responsibility to Cynthia.

"Let's take a preliminary vote to see where we stand in reaching a decision. I know this is a heavy burden, but we agreed we could determine the facts and reach a decision based on the evidence. Everyone here knows our decision could mean the death penalty for the defendant, Mr. Chang. We all have pads and pens. Tear off a piece of paper and write Y for yes or N for no and U for undecided. Do not write your names. This is only a straw vote to see how we proceed," stated Cynthia.

They passed all the slips of paper to the forewoman. Carefully she unfolded each one, placing the Y's on her left, the N's on her right, and the U's in the center. She announced each one as she sorted them.

"We have our work cut out for us. Ten for guilty, one for not guilty, one undecided. "

Grumbles and derogatory comments followed the tally of their informal vote. After days of sitting in the courtroom, several jurors were eager to resume their lives. The jurors scanned each face, familiar after days of sitting together, trying to determine who the holdouts were. The jurors who had voted guilty could not understand who could think Chang had not murdered Ruby. And after listening for days to the witnesses and the attorneys, who could still be undecided?

"Calm down." Cynthia raised her voice, slapping her hand on the table. "I will not tolerate disobedience. We are adults and we will act as adults, not like the thirteen-year-olds I teach."

"Whoa. We're adults here and don't have to be bossed around like teenagers," juror number five, the banker, said.

"Then stop acting like thirteen-year-olds," Cynthia said.

Juror number seven straightened. The sharp edge in her voice pierced him like a drill sergeant.

"See, I told you she would be good," Donna whispered to Beverly.

"How the hell can whoever voted N or U think that way? It's plain as day, he's guilty," shouted a juror.

"Yeah," another agreed. More jurors chimed in, and the order in the room slid into rude comments and noisy discussions until Cynthia clapped her hands for attention.

"You chose me as foreperson. This behavior won't accomplish a thing. It will only prolong our time in this austere room." She waited until the loud voices became whispers. "Now that this is out in the open, we will hear in a courteous manner why N and U voted the way they did."

"I voted undecided," said Karen.

"And it's me, Ruth, who voted not guilty."

"Ah, women are always undecided. That's why men are the head of the house," mumbled Charlie.

"I said we'd hear from Karen and Ruth with courtesy and mannerly. That means not speaking out of turn or being disrespectful. We will discuss this as a panel and in order of juror number," said Cynthia. "I'll go to the judge if you want and tell him who is not cooperating."

Everyone shut up with Cynthia's threat.

"Alright, then. Let's start with you, Karen."

"I voted undecided because my husband, if you recall, was the Executive Pastry Chef at Frederico's Steak House in New York. He would always talk about when the pastry cart was brought to the table. Not everyone could decide and would ask if anyone wanted to share a pastry because there were too many to decide. Some liked plain cheesecake, some with chocolate, some with strawberries. There were at least fourteen varieties of cheesecakes on the menu. Same with cannolis. There are cannolis with chocolate, key lime, pumpkin spice, black forest and more. There is Sicilian cannoli where the shell is crisp and the filling contains marsala wine. My point is, as my husband said, 'There are always too many choices and yet they all must be there.' Same here. Lots of evidence on the cart and we have to decide which ones to consider and which ones to pass on. That's what I mean about being undecided."

"And I said not guilty," Ruth said. "Why? Because being a travel agent on Royal Palm Way in Palm Beach, one of the wealthiest locations in the world, my clients think they want to travel where they had in mind until I review with them all the pros and cons of where they thought they wanted to go. After our meeting, they often changed their point of view from where they first started thinking they would travel, and I booked them somewhere completely different. So, same as Karen indicated. I need a more thorough look at the evidence. I will change my vote to undecided like my clients when they come to me."

"See, this is good. The bottom line is simple. We need to look thoroughly at the evidence," Cynthia said.

"And review all the witnesses," said Donna.

"I agree with Donna," said Beverly.

"Let's get to it. I'll send a note to the judge. We want to see the evidence and read the witness statements again," Cynthia said.

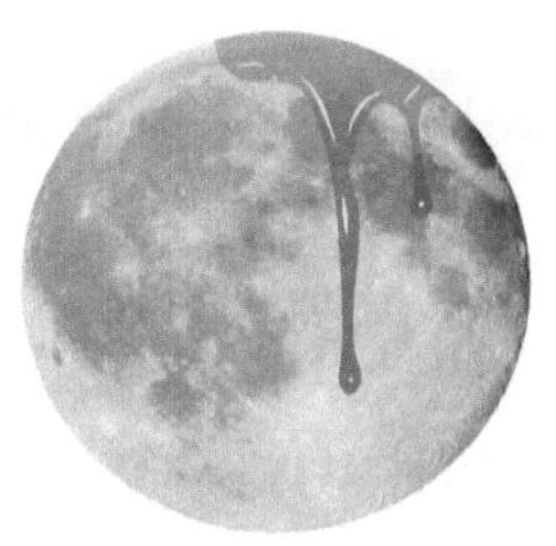

FORTY-FOUR

DAY 45
THE HACIENDA ARMS
LESTER'S PLACE

Lester kept his apartment exceptionally neat and uncluttered, seldom said of a single man living alone. Although he had a cleaning lady twice a month, he was a one of those people who had a place for everything and everything in its place ... even his women. Gloria was the exception, a hot-blooded Italian raised in a large family where the women stood their ground and demanded respect. Lester grew to like it and wondered if either of his two ex-wives had been like Gloria ... but who knows?

He plopped his felt Fedora hat atop the lamp shade next to his bed the day he moved in and it has stayed there as part of the décor.

"Lester, let me see. Turn here," Gloria said, placing the hat on Lester's head. "Let me fix this. That's it, a rakish angle. Now you're like Frank, only you have hazel eyes which I like better than blue," Gloria said as they lie naked from the night's lovemaking.

"Ah, Frank Sinatra, smooth and confident," Lester said.

"You're always smooth and confident. Stand up. Let me see."

"Stand up naked with my hat on? No."

"Just like a man with the customary no. Now, make your no, my yes. C'mon Lester, for me. It's a come as you are party," she said, laughing. "I'm getting Calliope. Stand up and play something for me," Gloria said as she left to fetch his trumpet.

Lester's head turned, and his gaze lingered on her ass, captivated by her extraordinary beauty. She possessed an allure that transcended mere mortal beauty. Her features were flawless, her nakedness sculpted with grace. She commanded attention effortlessly, more than his two ex-wives, Ramona from Lola's Jazz Club, or the few times he fucked Lorraine, the murdered judge's wife.

At first, he thought, *This broad's crazy, but I love it. Look at her. How can I refuse this Venus?*

She handed him Calliope. He got up, standing naked and, wearing his fedora, put his lips to the embouchure. Watching him tongue his mouthpiece, she imagined him using his tongue on her. Slowly, she drifted toward him like a purring cat on a slow prowl. She held Lester from behind, placing her head on his shoulder, her arms embraced his muscular physique. She felt his chest rise and fall as he played. The warmth of their nakedness at this moment, with nothing between them except the wonderful scent of Lester's cologne–along with the soft, melodic notes, made her desire him ever so more.

Gloria moved on him the moment Lester played the last note, removing Calliope from his hand. Lester turned and put his fedora on Gloria.

"You send a lightning bolt through my veins," and guided him to the bed. "Lie down."

Lester complied, just like her command to play Calliope and wear his fedora. He knew his prize.

"I don't know what it is lately. You, you, make me quiver," she said with the ardent skill of his hands.

Gloria's hands moved along his flanks, positioning herself. Her back arched, inviting him to her. The morning was theirs and no one else's. Not Frenchie, not

Yu, or Chang, not Lieutenant Walker, not the Abracadabra Studio, and certainly not Pamela's tarot cards.

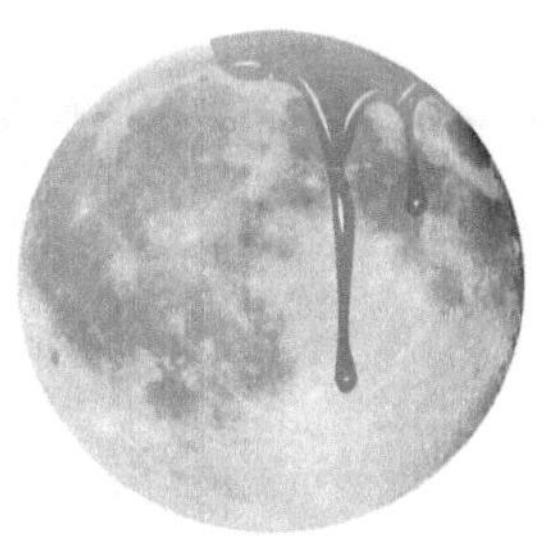

FORTY-FIVE

| LESTER CAINE INVESTIGATIONS

As usual, Louise had the morning coffee brewing. The fresh rich Columbian aroma wafted in the hallway, calling to her gal friends in adjacent offices on the same floor. Often, they would casually stop by for a brief coffee clutch. The baked cakes Louise picked up each morning from Rosie's Bakery were fresh and warm from the bakery. She and the office gals would eat, not fearing potential damage to their figures. In the few moments spent together, their stimulating conversations always gravitated towards their love lives and how exciting Louise's office was compared to their prosaic offices. The fact was, and Louise knew, they were there to see

Lester. His reputation while on the NYPD as the romance novel cover cop with his chiseled jaw, hazel eyes, and cleft chin had followed him to Palm Beach.

"Good morning, ladies," Lester said, entering.

"Good morning, Lester," they cooed in unison, each one craning their necks to follow his swagger as he passed, including Louise.

Gloria was just steps behind him.

"Alright girls, back to your plebeian offices, chop chop." She clapped her hands. Take your coffee and donuts with you. Bring back the cups."

They knew not to fuck with Gloria and silently turned, exiting single file.

"Lester, there's a message from Lieutenant Walker on top. He said it's important," Louise said, bringing him his coffee.

"Thank you, Louise. Ask Gloria to come in."

"Oh, Lester, good morning," Gloria mimicked in a high-pitched girly tone, mocking the visiting ladies.

"Give it a rest, Gloria. Let them get off on it, go home to their husband, boyfriends, or whomever, and fantasize." *Jesus, what would she do if she caught me with Ramona or Lorraine?*

"Put Walker on speaker," Gloria ordered, perching on the corner of Lester's desk, assuming the spot Louise usually took.

"Lieutenant Walker, Homicide," Ron answered in his usual monotone.

"It's Lester, Ron. Is the jury back?"

"No, and that's not a good sign. We are in day three of the deliberations and the last thing they asked for were the transcripts."

"Well, you never know. Maybe they're being meticulous. With six women on the jury, checking every detail," Gloria said.

"What, you think men would be slipshod? What say you, Lester?" Ron asked. "You've waited for a lot of jury decisions."

"Your guess is as good as mine. Maybe Gloria has something. Could be the women are very detail oriented. There are six of them. That's fifty percent of the jury, Ron," Lester answered. "But ..."

"But what?" Walker asked impatiently.

"But, you never know. From what I remember from voir dire, the women chosen seemed strong and independent. I didn't get any sympathizers from their interviews. Did you, Gloria?" Lester said.

"No, I didn't."

"My opinion is that women are against the death penalty. You know, bleeding hearts. Well, not you, Gloria, but the majority are," Walker stated.

"I take that as a compliment, Lieutenant. Thank you," she said.

"You both will be around for the verdict, won't you?" Walker asked.

"We're not going anywhere, Ron. Wouldn't miss it," Lester said.

They heard the loud click of Walker's disconnect through the speaker.

FORTY-SIX

| BUSY LIZZY AIN'T SO DIZZY

Elizabeth Thomson, one of the dinner guests on Ruby's last night alive, had asked Lester to call her Lizzy. She arrived at Lester's office.

Louise buzzed Lester on the intercom. "Lester, Mrs. Thomson is here to see you."

Lester pressed the button on the intercom for Louise to pick up the receiver so they could speak privately.

"She doesn't have an appointment, does she?"

"No," she answered.

"Did she say what it's about?"

"No, shall I—"

"It's alright. Send her in," he snapped, silencing Louise.

"Well, Mrs. Thomson, this is a surprise. What brings you here?"

"Did you forget? It's Lizzy. May I sit?"

"Of course. Shall I ask Gloria or Louise to sit in? Is this a case you want me to handle for you?"

"No, Lester. I wanted to thank you."

"For?"

"You remember I had the keys to Ruby's trailer, don't you? Clarence, the security guard, interrupted us. Well, I thought …"

"You're married, Lizzy."

"I'm not married anymore. I'm divorced now. You put me on to how and why I had the keys to Ruby's trailer. I found them in my husband's suit before I dropped it off to the dry cleaner. You suggested they were having an affair, and now I'm a single Palm Beach socialite. So, I was thinking we could—"

"Hello Mrs. Thomson," Gloria said, entering Lester's office after a signal from Louise.

"Gloria. Join us," Lizzy said without hesitation, although caught in an awkward moment.

Lester coughed, hiding a smirk behind his hand, knowing exactly why Gloria appeared.

"I was telling Lester that I'm divorced. Mr. Thomson and Ruby Russell were having an affair meeting in her trailer. That's how I could get in with Lester," she said, glaring at Gloria.

"Yeah, the day we were at the Abracadabra Studio memorial for Ruby. Mrs. Thomson—"

"Lizzy, Lester."

" Lizzy wanted to show me Ruby's trailer, in case there was more evidence. I didn't mention it because my search was interrupted," Lester said, not willing to risk Gloria's ire.

"The security guard came almost as soon as we got there and he made us leave," Lizzy said.

"So, do you have a case or business you want us to handle?" asked Gloria.

"No, I just wanted to say thank you."

"Alright, let's have a drink," Lester said, taking out the bourbon and three glasses. "We'll drink to your new circumstances."

"I like to celebrate," Lizzy said. "Anything further on Ruby's case?"

"The State rested its case against Chang and the jury is out for deliberations in the first-degree murder trial. Haven't you read the papers or watched the evening news?" Lester asked. "Frenchie and Chang's sister are nowhere to be found. She embezzled $1,000,000 of the studio's money from Ruby's account. Any idea where they may be? "

"Why, no. Why would I know? I just got back from Europe, celebrating my divorce from that…" Hesitating, she took a gulp of her whiskey. "Ruby and I were friends only on a social level after handling her divorce, as I told you."

"Well, now you know. If anything comes down the pike, you will let us know, won't you?" Gloria said.

"Of course, dear. Why wouldn't I? Lester, pour me another."

FORTY-SEVEN

DAY 52
DAY SEVEN OF JURY DELIBERATIONS

The phone rang one time. Louise jumped to answer, anticipating a call that the jury was back.

"Lester Caine Investigations, Louise speaking. How may I help you?"

The voice on the other end was short and to the point. "Jury's in." Click, then a dial tone.

Louise buzzed Lester, then Gloria. "Jury's in."

When Lester had opened his office, he chose a location strategically near the courthouse, attorneys, and bail bondsmen. He knew they would throw a lot of business his way. And so it had.

Lester and Gloria rushed out of the office and took the stairs, foregoing the old elevator with the brass scissor gate door. The occupants had to pull it shut after the outer door closed in its own good time. The courthouse was just around the corner.

"All rise. Hear ye, hear ye. The Circuit Court for the 15th District of Palm Beach County is in session–the Honorable Henry Wadsworth presiding. All having business before this honorable court draw near, give attention, and you shall be heard."

"You may be seated," said the judge. "Bring in the jury."

The jury filed in, taking their respective seats.

"Has the jury reached a verdict?" the judge asked.

The jury foreperson, Cynthia, stood. "We have, Your Honor."

A hush fell over the crowd.

"Bailiff, please bring me the verdict," the judge said. He opened the sealed envelope and read the missive slowly.[13] Folding it, he handed it to the Bailiff to return to the jury foreman.

______

[13] The judge will read the verdict before the foreman in court to prevent the possibility of misunderstandings and any appellate issues with the judgment or sentencing.

"The defendant will rise," said Judge Wadsworth.

Lei Chang and his attorney stood. Following protocol, two sheriff's deputies approached and stood behind Chang.

"Madam Foreman, please read the verdict," commanded the judge.

"Yes, your honor. We, the jury, in the State of Florida vs. Lei Chang, find the defendant guilty of the charge of murder in the first degree."

The cheers and jeers, hollering and weeping, following the decision echoed into the hallway, turning heads as they walked by.

"QUIET! ORDER IN THE COURT!" Judge Wadsworth pounded his gavel on the sounding block. "Quiet, or I'll have you removed," he said, alerting the sheriff's deputies at their stations. Whispered conversations replaced the pandemonium until the spectators fell silent. The deputies took Chang's hands, placing them behind his back. The click of the handcuffs closing on his wrists was loud in the courtroom.

"Is that the verdict of one and all?" the judge asked.

"Yes, Your Honor it is," she said.

"Your Honor, I would like the jury polled," Chang's attorney said.

"So granted. Is this the verdict of each of you individually? Go ahead please," Judge Wadsworth directed the jury.

One by one, each affirmed the decision with a resounding "yes."

"We will set the sentencing thirty days from now. Attorneys mark your calendars. Thank you, jurors, for giving your time and your service to our community. Go with God," the judge said, dismissing the jury.

"Court is adjourned." His gavel hitting the sounding block marked the end of the trial.

As the sheriff's deputies escorted him from the courtroom, Chang screamed, "I'll get you, Caine. This is not over."

FORTY-EIGHT

LESTER CAINE INVESTIGATIONS

Lester went into the office on Saturday, which he did occasionally to check the calendar for upcoming events. Besides, Gloria was at her place. She said she had 'to feed the cat,' although she doesn't have a cat. It's her way of getting her mail, doing laundry, paying bills, and a little personal time, making sure her place is in order since she spends so little time there.

Lester dialed the answering service.

"Mr. Caine, I have several messages. Do you want me to read them to you?"

"Sure, and I'll tell you which ones to pass to Louise. Go ahead."

As she read them off, he said; "Louise," meaning give them to Louise on Monday. Then she got to the last one. "You had a call late last night from Freddy. I tried to reach out to him for more information, but he said, 'Just tell Mr. Caine that Freddy called.' Then he hung up."

"That's fine. I know who he is. You can ignore that one. I'll handle it. Thank you."

"You're welcome, Mr. Caine. Anything else?"

"No, thank you." Lester hung up and immediately called Freddy at his private number, the Silver Slipper Supper Club. Freddy practically lived there.

Lester and Freddy Two Fingers were acquaintances from years past, when they were both in New York. Before Lester moved to homicide, he investigated a shootout. While conducting Mob business, Freddy had two fingers shot off. As a result, he gained the nickname Freddy Two Fingers.

There were no witnesses to the shooting and Freddy didn't want an ambulance, so Lester released the scene. He cleared everyone and drove Freddy to the hospital. Freddy never forgot it and regarded Lester as a stand-up guy. No one ever found out who shot Freddy, but Lester knew. The police never located the shooter and couldn't charge anyone without a body. If Lester had disclosed the shooter, Freddy would go to prison.

Freddy returned the favor over the years by providing information Lester couldn't have accessed, like Mob information or connections to someone in prison. He would not have been privy to inside information ordered by Mob Boss, Freddy Two Fingers, leaked information that helped Lester crack a case. It was Freddy Two Fingers who supplied the needed information Lester needed to identify the Nazi War Criminal he and Gloria hunted from Florida to Argentina and back to Florida.

During World War II, the Feds feared Mussolini's enemy supporters would sabotage the ports on the Eastern seaboard. The Italian Mob controlled the waterfront and Freddy Two Fingers controlled the Mob. Freddy cooperated with United States Naval Intelligence, helping FBI agents get union cards so they could work undercover on the New York docks.

Lester and Gloria knew well the Silver Slipper Supper Club in Miami and its owner. The fame of the club's blue crab meatballs and spaghetti was second only to the frequent appearances of the Hollywood elite. At one time, Ruby Russell frequented the club with other A-list box office actors and actresses, New York Broadway performers, and sports figures. Notorious mobsters from around the country, and on rare occasions from Italy, used the Silver Slipper as a top capo meeting place. It also served as a national message center for associated mob families.

Society romanticized about gangsters—feasted on photos showing them in a pool of blood, shot up in some restaurant. Freddy didn't allow photographers in the club, vetoed photos of his associates 'in the life,' as the gangsters referred to them, a phrase similar to a cop's description of 'on the job.'

Lester stopped his car and handed the young valet his keys and a five spot, confident that the young man would take personal care of his horizon blue Cadillac convertible.

One of Freddy's goons, as the tabloids called his henchmen, frisked Lester, removed his gat, and told him he'd get it back when he left. Another of Freddy's men escorted Lester to Freddy's private room, where Mob bosses from around the country and Italy met to discuss family business.

"Lester, welcome," Freddy said. He gestured to an empty chair. "Sit."

"Freddy," Lester acknowledged with a head bob. This wasn't a social call. Something he'd never do with a top Mob Boss. Freddy knew, too, theirs was strictly a business relationship.

"Ah, traveling light, I see. Where's your counterpart?" Freddy asked.

"She had business elsewhere," Lester said. Gloria despised Freddy and referred to him as a snake because he made her skin crawl. Lester kept her contact with him to a minimum. Safer that way … for both of them.

"So, I thought you two were going to tie the knot? I expected a wedding invitation."

"I'll send it to you by carrier pigeon," Lester said.

"Ah, Lester. That brings back memories," Freddy said.

"What does?"

"My homing pigeons. Back in the Bronx on the rooftop with my pigeon coops. They were loyal; always came home. I really enjoyed them."

"Isn't that the roof where Ralph the Trucker made like a bird and flew off the roof?" Lester said.

"Hmm. Somebody told me he thought he could fly like a pigeon. People do crazy things, Lester. Crazy things." He shook his head. "I didn't ask you here to hash over old times. Let's order," Freddy said, signaling his aide to bring his favorite dish for them, the Executive Chef's world class blue crab meatballs and spaghetti dish and Cabernet Sauvignon wine.

"Okay, Freddy. What do you have for me?"

"Lester, a little patience, less hostility. We've traveled a long way, go back a long time together. You know, quid pro quo. I thought you might want to know who you killed in that shootout. You know, the mug that waited for you and that dame from Lola's Jazz Club?"

"Jesus, Freddy. Does anything get by you? Yes, that would be good to know."

"Anthony Giovanni," Freddy said with a smirk. "You remember him?"

"You bet. Son-of-a-bitch. He must have lost a hundred pounds and grew a mustache—or tried to grow one. He was an underling to one of the New York families, as I recall. People knew him as Tony the Butcher for how he dismembered people for Don DiGrosso, one of your Goombas."

"He was a good soldier for the family." Freddy pressed his hand to his chest, but Lester didn't buy it.

"I put this guy behind bars for eighteen years. So, it was a revenge hit. Thanks for the info and the dinner invite, but I'm not hungry. I'll just take a Jim Beam," Lester said, lighting up a smoke.

Wait till I tell Ron. Anthony Giovanni is Mustache Pete. Mystery solved!

FORTY-NINE

| TESTA'S PLACE

Testa's Place on Royal Poinciana Way was a favorite breakfast spot for Lester and the local citizens, including Lieutenant Walker. Celebrities who frequented Testa's stayed at the Floridian Hotel on Palm Beach. They mingled with the local clientele, where they relaxed, undisturbed, between movie shoots. Because of the mild Florida winters, sports franchises established training facilities there. They frequently saw sports figures eating at Testa's while getting in shape for the season opener.

Lester, Gloria, and the locals came for the food with its stellar service. Gloria said all the photos of the celebrities and sports figures hanging on the walls around the restaurant made it seem ghostly. That's why she and Lester sat on the patio. You could smell the fresh ocean breeze and avoid the eyes watching you from the photos lurking above.

Lester always ordered for them both–Testa's perfect Eggs Benedict served with coffee and a Bloody Mary. The serving staff knew what Lester would order and immediately brought a pair of tomato juice-vodka drinks, replacing the stalk of celery with an extra shot of vodka before their breakfast arrived.

"Lester, Gloria. Good morning to you both. Hope all is well with you. If I knew you were coming, we could have sat together. That still wouldn't take the place of the steak dinner you owe me," Lieutenant Walker said.

"Fancy meeting you here, Ron. Care to join us?" Lester said, with Gloria adding her brief ado, "Lieutenant."

"No. I'm on my way out. Some of us have commitments and regular hours. I hope you cashed that big check you got as the reward. I got the collar and you got the big bucks," Walker said.

"Why?" Lester asked.

Walker lay down the morning *Miami Journal* newspaper stating, "Your favorite news gal, Helen Tilly, put you on the front page."

Gloria opened the paper, turning it so they could both read the headlines:

MOST WANTED KILLER ESCAPES JAIL BEFORE SENTENCING.

Will he make good the revenge he swore in Judge Wadsworth's courtroom? "I'll get you, Caine. This is not over," Chang screamed as deputies led him from the room. Lester Caine, Private Eye, and his associate, Gloria Saville, captured and returned Chang to Palm Beach to stand trial after he fled to avoid prosecution for the murder of glamorous movie star Ruby Russell.

"Jesus Christ," Lester exclaimed. "Are you kidding me, Ron? What the hell happened?"

"Settle down. You'll cause a ruckus, and the police will show up. Oh, never mind, they're here," Glória said, smiling at Lieutenant Walker.

"Out of my hands, Lester. He was the property of Palm Beach County Corrections until his sentencing date and transfer to prison. Then you know what was going to happen after that. Appeal after appeal that would run into years before they finally strapped him in to Old Sparky. I guess you didn't know, along with a lot of others," Ron said.

"Know what?"

"Your boy, Chang, here," Walker said, tapping the front page of the newspaper, "is a heroin addict. Corrections brought him to county detox after he had a legitimate seizure. He faked another one, knowing that a female Corrections Officer was at the desk alone that night. She opened the cell and wham! He sliced her from ear to ear with a makeshift shank, and she bled out. He's gunning for you, Caine. With the Corrections Officer's blood on his hands, he's subject to the fugitive law now. He knows he's a target, and he's out of control. Who knows? He could be a serial killer. There could be more bodies we don't know about and never will," Walker said.

"I'm calling Louise and telling her to keep Edith close and lock the door," Gloria said, getting up.

"Good idea, Gloria. Put her on guard, although I sent a car with uniforms to babysit your office. You know he'll try to get even before he flees. You heard him when they escorted him out of the courtroom. He's not done with you, Caine," Ron said.

"Thanks, Ron," Lester said.

"Okay. Louise said there is an officer in the hall and one in the car," Gloria said, returning to the table. "Thank you, Lieutenant. There's no telling what this stronzo will do."

Walker just looked at Gloria with furrowed eyebrows.

"It's an Italian expression for a person who is incompetent. No, no, more of an asshole," Gloria stated.

"Well, you enjoy the rest of the morning. Watch your back, Caine. I'm still waiting for that steak dinner you promised me."

"Ron, I promise."

"Why don't you bring your wife, Lieutenant? We'll make a night of it … dinner and a show at the Tuscany Hotel. Billie Holiday is there all month. Lester played his trumpet with her in the New York jazz clubs on 52nd Street. Maybe he can introduce us," Gloria said.

"Sounds like a great night. I'll tell my wife. Billie Holiday, Lester? You have a closet full of secrets."

Lester wondered. *How the hell did Walker's steak dinner become a double date?*

"We'll talk about it. Thanks for the heads-up, Ron."

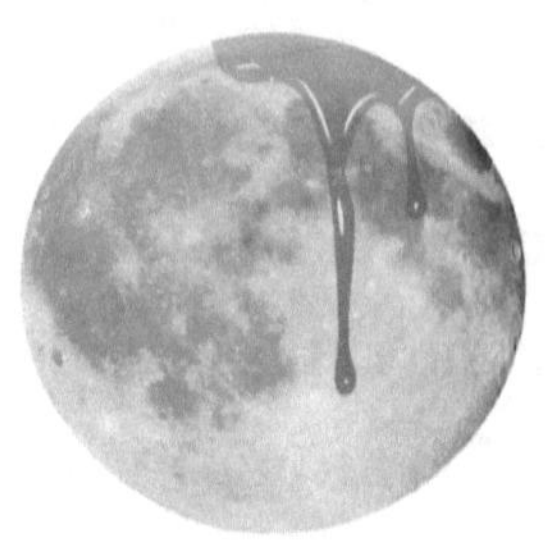

CHAPTER

FIFTY

Lester thought it best that Gloria and Louise bunk at his place until Chang was in custody again. From her first glance at the *Miami Journal* headline, Gloria had planned to do so. Louise could crash on Lester's Castro Convertible pullout bed. It would be tight sharing the bathroom with two women, but it was for the cause, as Lester put it. And Louise was beside herself, hoping, praying, she might get a glimpse of Lester's full Monty, if not more, not caring that Gloria was there or not. Maybe even a love tryst.

"Louise, I know you can handle yourself at the office, but I could hire a Pinkerton besides the uniforms," Lester said, as the morning began.

"Thank you, Lester. I think I'll be alright. If Chang is going to do what he threatened, it will be when it's dark, not during the daylight. The uniform cops are kinda cute. You never know," Louise smiled and winked. "Besides, Chang wants you, Lester."

"What do you have up your sleeve, Lester?" Gloria asked.

"You must still have contact with your snitches," Louise said.

"Now that the war is over, a lot of shipments are passing through the opened ports, making it a lot easier to smuggle opium and poppy plants to make morphine and produce heroin. Wounded soldiers' need for morphine during the war caused a shortage of poppy plants," Lester said. "Not anymore. I know some C.I.s. You do too, Gloria. We have to hit the streets to find the heroin dens," Lester said.

"I'll call my sisters. I know they can dig up some leads," Louise said.

"After we get to the office, it's Miami time. The plants are imported from Europe and go to various outlets before hitting the U.S. From there, the product goes to drug labs where they produce the final product—heroin. So, I bet Miami is a mega port for imports. We're going to start there. I know some places. Get ready, both of you. Who has dibs on the bathroom first?"

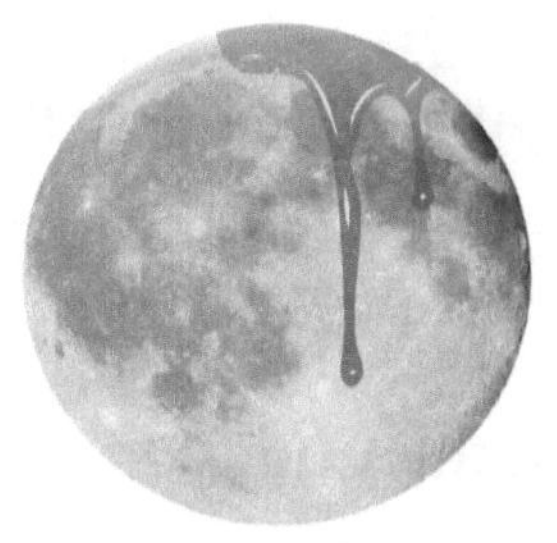

CHAPTER

FIFTY-ONE

Miami earned the nickname the Magic City, not because many people magically and mysteriously disappeared in the Everglades, but because of its growth and jobs: manufacturing plants, hotels, illegal and legal gambling with the ponies at Hialeah Park Racetrack, prostitution, mobsters, beautiful beaches, and pleasant year-round weather. The city was magic, exactly as it was called.

The Magic City's proximity to the Everglades earned the 1.5 million acres of wetlands a reputation as the dumping ground for undesirables, double crossers, welchers, and hoods who tried to outsmart the Mob.

Teeming with alligators, snakes, the Florida panther, and other predators, bodies disappeared. The remains never found.

Lester had driven the Caddy to Miami so many times he often said, 'This Caddy could drive itself there.' Frequently, they visited Miami on business, stakeouts, or to meet Freddy Two Fingers at the Silver Slipper Supper Club. They had spent considerable time in the Magic City and the surrounding suburbs while hunting the Nazi War criminal, Kurt Voker.

Lester knew the parts of town where most of the crime took place. Because of his training and twenty-five years with the NYPD and solving over two hundred homicides, he could have navigated to the shadowy streets with his eyes closed. Today was different. They weren't using his Caddy because it would stand out like the ringmaster in a three-ring circus. Lester's Caddy would draw the attention of every criminal he passed in the seedy parts of town. Today, hey drove Gloria's 1941 Ford business black coupe, less intrusive, fitting in with the black automobiles of the criminal element.

"Lester, I have my gun on my lap. You should have yours at the ready."

"I'm one step ahead of the shoeshine, Gloria."

"Good thing we know what we're doing. I've been to places like this when I was Military Police. We went into some pretty nefarious places to pull our men out of danger. I'm sure you have, too, both in the Navy and the NYPD," Gloria said.

"I can't tell you how many times I thought I might not make it out. Some places had seemed more dangerous than when I was with the Naval Unit, fighting those damn Banana Wars in the Dominican Republic, even leaving my blood in the soil there. Or the time I was undercover and wound up in the hospital for two weeks. The narc dealers' guards beat the shit out of me just to be sure I wasn't undercover. Little did they know every fucking one of them would wind up in prison."

"You told me you got shot. I see the medals hanging in the office every day."

"The good, the bad and the ugly," Lester said.

"Slow up here and park. Let's get out. We can walk and see if anyone recognizes Chang." Gloria said.

They strolled. Both had their rods at the ready. Gloria asked each hooker working the streets, waiting to service their next John.

"Have you seen this man?" Showing Chang's photo. "He's my brother. I need to find him." One after the other, along with the derelicts lying in the doorway, they shook awake to show Chang's photo. All of them in a trancelike stupor from drugs and alcohol, many too out of their minds to answer until …

"Yeah, I seen him, a lot of him, if you know what I mean. He paid me for my professional services. He thought he was great, doing me a favor. I played along. You know, he's my john. So I do him. Those Asian men are-small, not like you, a real man," placing her hand on Lester's chest. "He finished and went his way, and I went mine. You don't look Chinese. And I don't give a damn. I might tell you where he hangs and gets his fix, but you're takin' up my time here," she said, staring up at Lester's hazel eyes.

"Okay, honey, hands off," Gloria said.

Lester broke out a five-spot, closing her hand around it.

"Lady, you got some guy here. You better take care of him. Five bucks. Thanks, mister. If you ever come back alone, I'll give you a free ride. You'll be in for a good time," she said.

"Hey," Gloria snapped. "You got more than you'd get from a john. Give with the details. Where's my brother?" Gloria said through gritted teeth.

"Two blocks east to Spring Street. Make a right and in the middle of the block is a hotel. You can rent rooms by the hour, day or week. You'll fit right in there the way you're dressed. I have a room if you are interested in using it. But, you know, that'll cost you too," she said.

HOTEL OPAL

"She was right on target with where the hotel is. Let's hope the five-spot pays off," Lester said.

"I can't imagine what the owner was thinking, naming this hotel like the semi -precious opal gemstone." Gloria said.

"What did you expect for a rent-by-the-hour place? It's a fucking dump. Let's do it," Lester said.

They approached the desk clerk hiding behind the glass barrier he hoped would protect him from the street element. Maybe, maybe not.

How far down on your luck do you have to get to take a job like this? Lester wondered, looking the loser over with a touch of pity. Stink permeated the air not only from neglected maintenance and basic cleaning, but from the stale sex that accompanied the hookers leaving after their tour of duty.

They entered with their palms on their rods, flashing their P.I. credentials. Gloria held up Chang's photo.

"Where is he? What room?" she snarled.

"Don't pick up that phone and call him if you want to use your fingers again," Lester said.

"Detective, there ain't no such thing as a phone in these here rooms. He's in room nine. Up the stairs to the right," the clerk said. "I ain't doin' nuthin'; I don't see nuthin'; or hear nuthin'," he said.

Silent, like a cat, they climbed each step, every one squeaking a protest as they stepped on it. A hooker and her client passed them on the stairs. The john pulled his hat low, concealing his face, as he left with her. They reached the door to number nine and stopped. Lester put his ear to the door.

"Nothing," Lester whispered. Holding up three fingers, Gloria tensed, knowing exactly what was going down when the last finger dropped—break the door in.

Lester's fingers folded one by one. He busted the flimsy door in by kicking the weakest spot near the keyhole next to the lock. It blew in like a paper airplane in flight.

Chang tumbled from his bed, dazed, not immediately grasping what was going on.

"Hands up. There's nowhere to go. Don't be stupid," Lester said.

"Keep your hands where we can see them," Gloria added.

"You may have me, but you'll never find Frenchie or Yu. They are far away with all that money. Money like neither of you will ever see."

"Neither will you," Lester said.

"Even if you find where they are, there's no extradition from that country, so go fuck yourself," Chang said, diving for his gun under the pillow. He brought it out in one swift motion.

BLAM! BLAM! BLAM! BLAM! BLAM!

Shots rang out from Lester's and Gloria's guns. Hotel occupants ran past the broken door, like roaches scattering when the lights came on.

"I'm good," Lester said. "You?"

"Me too," Gloria said. "So, if it's true, Frenchie and Yu are living the good life in some foreign country with no extradition to the United States."

"I remember from my days at the NYPD there are at least ten of them. It would be like looking for that proverbial needle in a haystack, searching ten countries."

"Well, Lester, Pamela's tarot cards were right again. Here is the *Chariot Card:* triumph, victorious, overcoming obstacles and the finale—conquest," Gloria said.

"Here lies our conquest, riddled with bullet holes on a blood-soaked mattress. Let's call it in," Lester said.

LIST OF CHARACTERS

MAIN:

Lester Caine-
Gloria Saville
Louise-
Amélie Dubois- (Frenchie)
Lei Chang-
Ron Walker-Palm Beach Police Lieutenant

CAMEOS:

Miguel Gonzalez-Gardener at the Ruby Russell Palm Beach Estate.
Helen Tilly-reporter for the Miami Journal.
Warner Oland and Sidney Toler-Both movie actors portraying Private Eyes Charlie Chan in 1930's & 1940's.
Roger Puglia-President of Abracadabra Studios.
Jonathan Deinhart-President of Quarter Moon Productions.
Pamela-Lester's mother
Ramona-bar keep and Lester's lover

Mustache Pete-Anthony Hatchell Giovanni- apo for the DiGrosso crime family in New York.

Lola-owner of Lola's Jazz Club

Claudette-singer at Lola's Jazz Club and one time Lester's lover

Carl-barkeep at Lola's Jazz Club

Lorraine-murdered Judge Desmond Vanderbilt's widow (Book One-Lester Caine Private Eye, Murder on Palm Beach)

Kurt Voker-Nazi War Criminal, who adopted the name Leopold Israel Rabinowitz to escape Germany. (Book ___

Al & Marcia-owners of Alvi's Paint and Hardware store.

Yu Yīng-Lei Chang's sister

Clarence-Back lot security guard at The Abracadabra Studios

Mrs. Caserta-Pamela, Lester's mother's neighbor.

Freddy Two Fingers-Mob Boss

Henry Wadsworth -Circuit Court Judge for Lei Chang trial.

Jurors:-Jonathan, Harold, Cynthia, Ruth, Donald, Ross, Richard, Judi, Charles, Donna, Beverly. Karen.

DINNER GUESTS:

Miss Beverly Hart–Miss Russell's Palm Beach decorator.

Mr. and Mrs. Bob Berman–City Councilman.

Mr. and Mrs. Ted Beasley–Palm Beach Mayor.

John Arthur–Stage and Screen Actor.

Mr. Walter Thomson– Real Estate developer

Elizabeth (Lizzy), Palm Beach divorce attorney, and Mr. Thomson's Wife.

WATSON:

-San Francisco FBI Agent.

NO NAMES:

Medical Examiner and Assistant

Limo driver-no name_

Housekeeper at Ruby Russell's

FBI agents

Cabbie

Maître D's.-The Forbidden City Nightclub and Cabaret and Shanghai Low

Dock guard

Chinese ship captain and armed guard

San Francisco Police Lieutenant

Florida Court Bailiff, Prosecutor, and Defense Attorneys.

Hooker in Miami.

A smokin' gun note to you, my readers. I thank you for reading my novel. You are exceptional!

A writer begins with a blank page. A reader, like you, helps me to finish it.

Please add a review or a simple 5 Star rating and let me know what you thought of Lester's latest adventure.

Reviews are extremely helpful for authors. Thank you for taking the time to support me and my work. Don't forget to share your review on social media with the #fredberri and encourage others to read the story.

You can add reviews on any of the following online retailers.

Amazon.

Barnes & Noble

Walmart

Books-a-Million

Kindle

Nook

Audible

Bookwire

Sincerely,

fred berri

*Don't forget to subscribe for advanced special offers,
bonus content, updates from author, fred berri and
info on new releases.*

Go To:
fredberri.com

REFERENCES

1 - Lester Caine's car. 1948 Cadillac

2 - Gloria Saville's 1941 Ford Business Coupe Series 62 Horizon Blue Convertible

Lester Cain's singing voice- fred berri

Judy Garland- an American actress and singer.

Frank Sinatra- an American singer and actor. Nicknamed the "Chairman of the Board" and later called "Ol' Blue Eyes", he is regarded as one of the most popular entertainers of the mid-20th century.

Duke and Dutchess of Windsor-The Duke of Windsor was a title in the Peerage of the United Kingdon. The Duke-Edward VIII and his wife, Bessie Wallis Warfield, The Duchess.

Clark Gable (William) Clark Gable- an American film actor. Often referred to as The King of Hollywood,

Page boy-(old fashioned) young boy or man, usually in uniform, employed in a hotel to open doors, deliver messages for people, etc.

Police radios & scanners- Communications remained public as two-way police transmissions became common in the 1940s. Radioed instructions like "be on the lookout" and "calling all cars" entered popular culture. Newspapers assigned cub reporters to monitor police scanners, listening for the next big story.

The Ruby Waltz-a song by J. Edgar Gould, 1875

City Councilman-part of the governing of the City that enacts ordinances subject to the approval or veto of the Mayor. The City Council orders elections, levies taxes, authorizes public improvements, approves contracts and adopts traffic regulations.

Errol Flynn (Errol Leslie Thomson Flynn)- an Australian-American actor who achieved worldwide fame during the Golden Age of Hollywood. He was known for his romantic swashbuckler roles.

Warner Brothers Studio- An American film production and distribution company known for its action feature films.

Abracadabra Film Studio- A fictitious Hollywood movie studio created by author fred berri for Ruby Russell's films.

***Billie Holiday*-** An American jazz and swing music singer and a very important influence on jazz and pop singers. How she sang was similar to the way jazz musicians played their instruments.

***Chick Webb* (**William Henry "Chick" Webb)- an American jazz and swing music drummer

***Coleman Hawkins* (**Coleman Randolph Hawkins, nicknamed "Hawk",)- an American jazz tenor saxophonist.

***Thelonious Monk*-** an American jazz pianist and composer with a unique improvisational style.

***Dick Tracy*-** an American comic strip featuring a tough and intelligent police detective like Lester Caine.

Radio City Music Hall & The Rockette Dancer's (Radio City Music Hall also known as Radio City)- an entertainment venue and theater in New York City. It is the headquarters for The Rockette Dancers.

***Dumdum Bullets*-** the name of the arsenal in India where the original hollow point bullets were produced in the late 19th century, thus 'dumdum' became the generic term for expanding bullets when hitting a target would make a mushroom style opening.

***Dick, Gumshoe*-** terms used for private detectives.

***Mustache Pete*-** a derogatory term for someone unwilling to embrace new ways due to their outdated notions of decency.

Doh-rey-mee (Do-re-mi)- slang for money

APB- All Points Bulletin is an electronic information broadcast sent to a group of recipients to communicate important information like, *wanted for murder.*

"Of all the gin joints in all the towns in all the world, she walks into mine."- A famous quote spoken by actor Humphrey Bogart who played Rick in the movie *Casablanca.* He says this line in a flashback scene while grieving over his ex-girlfriend's marriage. She appears in his nightclub. This line is considered one of the most romantic dialogues in movie history.

It Had To Be You- a popular song composed by Isham Jones, with lyrics by Gus Kahn.

Alvi's Paint and Hardware store- A fictious name & location created by Author fred berri.

Midget- is a term that was originally coined in 1865 referring to an extremely short person with limbs similarly proportioned to his body. The movie industry and circus used midgets in their movies and circus acts. It provided employment for individuals who otherwise could not get jobs. The medical field used this term until 1960. It was acceptable during the era of this novel.

AP- Associated Press produces news reports that distributes to newspapers, radio and TV broadcasts.

Craps- A dice game called because it is a spinoff of the French word *crapaud,* which means "toad"–referencing the original style of play where people would crouch over like a frog on the sidewalk.

Shanghai Low and Forbidden City- Were real Chinese American nightclubs in San Francisco's Chinatown in the 1940's.

Hack- from Chapter 23. Taxi drivers referred to as a "hack," originating from the term "hackney carriage," a horse-drawn carriage for hire as to hire out their carriage.

Beat me Daddy Eight to the Bar- It means 8 notes to the (usually) 4 beat bar, or measure, or twice as fast as the beat. Gloria was indicating she was twice as fast to think just what Lester was thinking--NOT that he was going to spank her.

Houdini (Harry Houdini)- a professional escapologist, illusionist, noted for his escape acts.

Swiss Bank Accounts- Switzerland at one time allowed bank accounts to be numbered without anyone's name on the accounts, allowing total anonymity so the spoils and robbery from the war could hide to avoid paying taxes.

"Six ways to Sunday"- used to mean "in every possible way, with every alternative examined. An early use: *The Chicago Tribune*, November 1925: "If you were a lawyer, you could say that six ways to Sunday, but it would all come to the same thing."

Naval Intelligence- United States government entity that went to Freddy himself during World War II to get FBI agents union cards to work the New York docks undercover is true. The real Freddy at the time was Charles "Lucky" Luciano. See Wikipedia; Collaborations between the United States government and Italian Mafia.

Testa's- An iconic and longest running restaurant in Palm Beach.

Floridian Hotel- A fictitious hotel in Palm Beach.

Old Sparky- Nick name for the electric chair used for executions.

Castro Convertible- Invented by Bernard Castro, the sofa that converted to a pullout bed.

The Full Monty- Originated from the tailoring industry in the 1900s. Anyone who bought a three-piece suit would have gone the "Full Monty." Thus, the works, the whole enchilada. That was certainly something Louise longed to see, Lester's whole enchilada.

Pinkerton- an American private independent police force and security company founded in 1850.

Acknowledgements

Publisher– frederic dalberri

Editor - jc konitz: https://rb.gy/f0ciy

Cover – Judith San Nicolas; judithsdesign.com

SPECIAL THANKS

to

JC Konitz

For helping with the naming of Ruby Russell.

Books by fred berri

Cousins' Bad Blood
Cousins' Bad Blood-The Take Over
Murder on Contadora Island

* * *

Books featuring Homicide Detective Johnny Vero
Ten Cents a Dance
Bullets Before Dawn-Murder in Chinatown
Sabre Blue Society

* * *

Books featuring Lester Caine-Private Eye
Murder on Palm Beach
Pigpen Cipher

* * *

Books featuring Adventures of Carmelo™
Swim Survival Lessons–The Dentist–The Eye Doctor–
Going to the Hospital–Jiu Jitsu–Summer Vacation–
Coloring Book

The Adventures of Carmelo™ is a series of children's learning stories. These stories help children understand new adventures, teaching respect, listening, following instructions, to be brave, and that it's okay to be scared when facing a new adventure.

Coming Soon:
Lester Caine Private Eye
The Sins of the Father

ABOUT THE AUTHOR

Mr. Berri graduated Columbia State University with a business degree. He volunteered teaching Junior Achievement in the Florida school district and led a volunteer reading program for grades K-3. He has done public speaking and appeared in TV commercials and voice overs. Berri has written numerous murder mysteries and children's books which can be found:

website: **fredberri.com**

Amazon

Barnes & Noble

Walmart

Books-a-Million

Kindle

Nook

Audible

And all online book sellers.

Five Star Award-winning Author

fredberri.com